Too late for protests too late for words

Every nerve in Cindy's body sprang to life with a yearning she would never have believed herself capable of. As Zac's eyes slowly roamed the length of her naked body, her pulses leaped as they did every time he touched her.

He didn't kiss her. He just looked at her and let his hands travel very, very lightly over her face, her throat, her shoulders, her breasts. She saw his eyes close, as though he would store indelibly in his mind every detail of her.

"Beautiful...." Zac's voice had roughened, deepened, so that it was barely recognizable. "You're incredibly, perfectly beautiful."

Cindy closed the distance between their bodies. Her blood was on fire, pounding through her veins. She was desperate for his kiss; her entire body trembled, screamed for his touch....

HARLEQUIN ROMANCES
by Claudia Jameson

These books may be available at your local bookseller.

For a free catalog listing all titles currently available, send your name and address to:

Harlequin Reader Service
P.O. Box 52040, Phoenix, AZ 85072-9988
Canadian address: Stratford, Ontario N5A 6W2

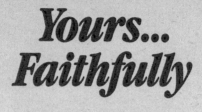

Yours... Faithfully

Claudia Jameson

Harlequin Books

TORONTO • NEW YORK • LONDON
AMSTERDAM • PARIS • SYDNEY • HAMBURG
STOCKHOLM • ATHENS • TOKYO • MILAN

Original hardcover edition published in 1983
by Mills & Boon Limited

ISBN 0-373-02594-7

Harlequin Romance first edition January 1984

For
PETER
with much love

CHAPTER ONE

'GONE? Fired? What do you mean, he's been *fired*? What on earth's been happening around here?' Cindy Hetherington lowered herself gracefully into her chair, bewildered by what she was hearing, by what she was seeing.

She was sitting in her own office, but she barely recognised the place. To say it had been given a face-lift while she'd been away on holiday would be putting it mildly. Not only did she find herself sitting at a new desk, on which there was a sleek new typewriter, she also found herself in a room in which two of the walls had been painted pillarbox red—a colour she would never have chosen in a million years! The new carpet was a mottled brown and beige. That, at least, was inoffensive, but the only things which were completely familiar in the room were Cindy's array of potted plants. Those and her young assistant, Alison.

'Alison?' Cindy's dark brown eyes looked questioningly at the younger girl but it was Sheila who answered. It was Sheila who had met Cindy at the entrance to the advertising agency's offices some five minutes earlier, and Sheila who had done all the talking so far.

'I've just told you! Your boss has been ousted! Sacked. Fired without ceremony. Paid off. Got rid of. I can't put it more plainly than that, can I?' Sheila hitched herself on to Cindy's desk, her long and spindly legs looking thinner than ever in a skirt which finished four inches above her knees. On a woman who looked more than her thirty-five years, that was pushing it a bit. And she'd had her hair cut again, Cindy noticed. Why did some women insist on following fashion in a sheep-like manner and never stop to consider what actually suited them? On

Sheila's pale, too-thin face her black hair cropped severely short looked ghastly.

Cindy half turned in her chair so she was no longer face to face with the offending pillarbox red on the wall. She sighed inwardly, wishing it had been someone other than Sheila who had greeted her with the news that the agency had been taken over. There was so much cynicism in Sheila that it was difficult to get a straight answer from her at the best of times.

Though they worked under the same roof, the two women saw little of one another. Sheila was a copy-writer. She kept her own hours, coming and going as she pleased, and worked well away from Cindy in the creative department on the far side of the building. In the course of her work, Cindy saw most of the advertising copy written by Sheila. She could write ads in so many different ways, from the persuasive to the humorous to the technical—depending on the product being sold—and it never ceased to amaze Cindy that anything other than satire could be produced by Sheila's pen.

Cindy didn't dislike her. Sheila was one of those people it was difficult to dislike. But she didn't exactly like her, either. There had to be a reason she was here, sitting in Cindy's office. There had to be a reason for her taking the trouble to come in early in order to collar Cindy before she'd even got through the main entrance to the offices. Or was it simply that she wanted to be the one who broke the news about the takeover?

'No, you can't put it more plainly.' Cindy shook her head, her blonde curls moving gently against the tanned skin of her shoulders. 'But how can my boss be fired? John was the Managing Director, for heaven's sake!'

'So what?' Sheila lit a cigarette, departing from her usual drollness into something bordering on excitement. She was grinning from ear to ear. 'John Doe might have been the Managing Director, but he had only one share in this agency. One share. Mr Bryant ran this place, not your boss. John Doe had about as much management ability as a juvenile flatfish.'

From behind her desk in the corner of the office, Alison giggled. She had been with Bryant's only two months, not long enough to have become used to Sheila's brand of wit and to the nicknames she gave everybody. She still found Sheila amusing, still found it hilarious when the M.D., the *ex* M.D., was referred to as 'John Doe'.

Cindy looked heavenward, her loyalty to John preventing her from making any comment, though there was a good deal of truth in Sheila's remark.

That the ownership of the agency had changed hands didn't really surprise Cindy. The Chairman, Mr Bryant, who had been the founder and backbone of the agency, was way past retirement age. His tiredness and increasing lack of interest in the business had been reflected in the staff, in the lethargy which had been creeping through the agency during the past couple of years.

In the past, Bryant's had been one of the best advertising agencies in London, but these days it was surviving on its old reputation. That and a diminishing amount of business. In the four years that Cindy had been there they had lost three accounts, old-established clients. And they had won no new ones. The agency was rapidly going downhill, and whoever had bought the place would have a difficult task in reversing that process. A very difficult task.

Of course John had been at fault, as much if not more than the ageing Mr Bryant. It was undeniably true that Cindy's boss had not been much of a Managing Director. Working as his secretary had taxed Cindy to less than half her potential. Oh, there had always been something to do, but the job had never been a challenge to Cindy. She'd never had the chance to use her brains, or all her qualifications. Nevertheless, she had liked her boss enormously, and it seemed incredibly cruel that he had been ousted so sharply by the new owners of Bryant's. She said as much to Sheila.

'Knickers!' Sheila gave her a withering look. 'The ad world is tough and ruthless. There's no room for sentiment—you should know that by now. You're too soft, Goldilocks, I've told you that before. I can't imagine why you ever came into this business in the first place.'

That was none of Sheila's business. Cindy had had good reasons for choosing the advertising world for her career, just as she'd had good reasons for leaving her home in Cheshire and wanting to live in the capital.

'Sheila, why don't you keep your questions and your opinions to yourself and just tell me, as objectively as you can manage, what happened here after I'd left for my holidays?' she said.

Sheila groaned in frustration, her eyes sparking with amusement. 'Heavens, *when* are you going to ask me who's bought this dump of a place?'

When Cindy didn't answer, Sheila threw up her hands in despair. 'Okay, Miss Cool, I'll tell you from the top.' She wiped the smirk from her face, wriggled herself into a more comfortable if unladylike position on Cindy's desk, and spoke to the younger woman as if she were hard of hearing. 'You left on the Friday, right? On the following Thursday a staff meeting was called. Are you with me so far? We all gathered in the Board Room and our decrepit Chairman announced that he'd sold all his shares. It was done! Fait accompli! As from last Monday, we were all working for someone else.' Sheila leaned forward slightly, her eyes narrowing. 'Those of us who've been allowed to stay on, that is.'

'What do you mean? Who else has been fired?' Cindy blinked in surprise, still bewildered by all this.

There followed a list of seven names. Seven members of the agency's staff who had been sacked. Paid in lieu of notice.

'Good grief!' Cindy leaned back in her chair, flabbergasted. 'But you can't do that! Not these days. You can't just——'

'In this business, darling, anything can happen.'

Sheila's laugh was scornful. 'And when you know who the new boss is, you'll understand.'

'But—but . . .' Cindy didn't know what to say. In one fell swoop some of the agency's key people had been removed. Just like that! 'I've never heard of anything like it! Not on this scale. I mean——'

'I have.' Sheila sounded almost triumphant. 'I've seen it happen before. About ten years ago, when I was working for——'

Alison was looking from one woman to the next, fascinated but unable to get a word in.

'Politics.' Cindy said the word with distaste. 'It's the old internal politics game, isn't it?'

Sheila shrugged. 'Partly. Strictly speaking, those seven weren't all fired. Five of them were. Everyone else was given the opportunity of staying on, but the two account executives walked out on the spot—as soon as they were told who the new boss was . . . Come on!' she urged. 'I'll give you three guesses who's taking over Bryant's.'

'I'm in no mood for guessing games. Why don't you just tell me before you burst?' Cindy let out a long, slow breath, unable to decide how she felt about all this. But the idea that she was now working for someone else rather appealed to her. Working for someone who would keep her busy, be more demanding than John, might help to lift her depression. She had been depressed before she left for her holidays, thanks to James, and after spending two weeks in her father's company she was even more depressed. She shook herself mentally, refusing to dwell on thoughts of her relationship with James.

Yes, a new boss might be just what she needed. Come to think of it, she hoped he would tax her to her fullest. It would be good to be busy again, as she used to be when she first started at Bryant's. She decided there and then that she would stay on. After all, with a new Chairman, a new Managing Director and several new members of staff, Bryant's was bound to undergo a drastic change—one way or another. It would be a new job for Cindy, without the necessity of looking elsewhere.

'And what about the other two Directors, Sheila? I mean, there was John and——'

Sheila waved a dismissive arm. 'They suffered the same fate as John—ousted. After all, they had so few shares between them, they had little choice but to sell. Mr Bryant owned eighty per cent of the shares, bear in mind.'

Cindy smiled to herself. She couldn't delay the question much longer. Having decided to stay on, she was now as curious to find out about the new owner as Sheila was anxious to tell her. 'All right, Sheila, let's have it. Who is our new Chairman?'

'Are you ready for this?'

'I'm ready.'

Sheila held out her hands with a flourish. 'Zac Stone! How about that?'

The announcement fell flat. Cindy didn't respond. For the moment, the name meant nothing to her. It was ringing a bell, but that was all.

Sheila let out an exaggerated moan. 'Good God, what's the matter with you? I think your holiday's given you moths in the brain! I've just told you that this place has been taken over by *Zachariah Stone*, and you sit there as if you're fast asleep with your eyes open!'

Two pairs of eyes were watching Cindy closely. Alison, able finally to get a word in, ventured, 'He's very nice, Cindy. I'm sure you'll like him.'

'Don't be silly, Alison!' Sheila turned round and snapped at the youngster. 'Nice is not a word that can be used when talking about Zac Stone. Not in any context. He's—er—let me see . . . he's *professional*.'

Cindy nodded slowly. She'd placed the name, all right. It had only taken her about five seconds. There was only one Mr Stone in the advertising world, but . . . 'But Zac Stone retired about two years ago, didn't he? I mean, when he sold his original agency, didn't he make some sort of agreement not to set up business elsewhere?'

'Well done!' Sheila's voice was sarcastic, but Cindy paid no attention. Sheila's sarcasm had never affected her. There was nothing personal in it. One just had to understand the woman. She was like that with everyone.

Cindy smiled tolerantly. 'Okay, we all know that if we want to find out anything about people on the advertising scene, we've only to ask you. So why don't you fill me in on the details of Zac Stone?'

Sheila pouted as if she'd been offended—something which was virtually impossible to do. 'You make me sound like a gossip and a scandalmonger!'

'No,' Cindy couldn't help laughing, 'I didn't mean to imply that. But you are a mine of information. You pick up *everything* that runs along the grapevine.'

'Just one of my virtues. Well, Zac Stone was the majority owner of Stone, Mason and Gibbons. That much you know. It was, and still is, the top agency in London. We all know the turnover of that agency, so you can imagine the price he got for it! Anyway, in the contract of sale, Zac agreed to keep off the advertising scene completely for at least one year—obviously the buyers didn't want him setting up business elsewhere and taking all his clients with him! After all, it was his name they were paying for. Anyhow, the story goes that Zac was retiring from working life altogether. At thirty-five, if you don't mind!'

At that, Alison spoke up. 'But if he sold his agency and retired, why has he come back two years later and bought this place?'

'Shut up, Alison, you may not ask questions I don't know the answer to!'

They laughed, all of them, as Sheila continued with what she did know about Zac Stone. 'I know nothing about him personally, except that he's Welsh. They say he started out working in an agency as a mailboy! Imagine it! He's come up the hard way. What he doesn't know about the ad world, and I mean every aspect of it, isn't worth knowing. He's the tops. He'll put this agency on its feet again. He's such——'

Sheila stopped in mid-sentence as the door opened and John Crosdale walked in. John worked in the accounts department. He was a sweet man, nicely spoken with impeccable manners, and Cindy liked him very much.

He stopped in his tracks when he saw Sheila sitting there. 'Oh!' He looked from Sheila to his watch, and frowned. 'I didn't expect——'

Cindy laughed. 'Sheila's broken a record, John. She wanted to be the first to tell me the news, I suppose.'

'And have you been told? I mean, have you been told who your new boss is?'

As John looked from one woman to the next, Sheila shrugged dramatically. ' 'Course I've told her! But you know Miss Cool isn't easily ruffled. She didn't even react!'

John smiled, though he didn't look at all happy. Not at all. 'You've probably never met Zac Stone, have you, Cindy?'

'No. But I know of him. I know his reputation. Who doesn't?'

'He's a bastard!' John said suddenly, vehemently. 'A bastard, first class.'

This was so out of character that Cindy's eyebrows shot up in astonishment. If John hadn't been so obviously upset, she might have laughed.

'Oh, I don't know about that,' Sheila said drily. 'Where did you hear that his parents never got married?'

'Spare me,' John said stiffly. 'Spare me the puns today, Sheila. Just let me get used to the idea that starting this week I'm going to have to work within Zac Stone's orbit!'

Cindy was a little puzzled. A little puzzled and very interested. 'You know Mr Stone, I take it?'

'Yes, quite well.'

'I've met him a few times,' Sheila began.

'It's not quite the same thing,' John cut in. 'You've never *worked* for him before. But you're working for him now, so you'll find out what he's really like. Give it time.'

'And you have?' Cindy probed. 'Worked for him, I mean?'

'Yes.' John smiled at her. But then he always had a smile ready for Cindy. Always. 'I worked at Stone, Mason and Gibbons—for a total of six months.'

'And you're staying on here?'

'I haven't much choice, have I, dear? I've got a mother and an aunt who depend on me. I'll see how it goes. If I can't stand it, I'll look for another job—but I'll do it at my leisure. When it suits me.'

There was a sudden silence. Alison looked round the room as if she were sorry the show was over. 'Well, I thought Mr Stone was very nice when he had a talk with me last week,' she proffered. 'Good-looking, too. And he's a bachelor!'

Everyone turned to look at Alison, but nothing was said. Not a word. Everyone was thinking their own thoughts. Alison, young for her eighteen years and basically very shy, blushed to the roots of her hair.

Cindy felt a rush of sympathy for her and distracted the other two as quickly as she could. 'Did you want something, John? Or had you come in to tell me the news?'

'The latter. I thought you should be warned.'

Cindy looked at her watch as John closed the door behind him. 'Alison, have we got any work to do? I mean, was there anything outstanding before John——'

Sheila clicked her tongue. 'You're not very subtle, Cindy. if you want me to go now, just say so.'

'I want you to go now.'

'Oh, that's charming! And I came in early especially to do you a favour. You haven't heard the rest of it yet.'

'You mean there's more?' Cindy looked at her in mock disdain. It was true that she wasn't easily ruffled. Cindy Hetherington was well spoken, well bred, well

educated and quietly confident. Whatever was ahead of
her in her working life, she would cope with it. She had
no doubts about her abilities. If she could only manage
her personal life as well as she managed her working
life, she'd be okay.

She looked up at Sheila coolly, her soft brown eyes
smiling from a face that was exceptionally lovely,
although she personally could find a dozen faults with
it. 'Go on, then. What's the rest of it?'

'Zac's the new Chairman *and* Managing Director.'

'I see.' The note of disappointment in Cindy's voice
was plain. 'And Mr. Bryant's secretary has been given
the job, is that it? Well, I suppose that's fair enough.
Miss Druce has been here nearly twenty years, after all.
Compared to my four.'

At last everything fell into place. So this was the
real reason for Sheila's presence. 'What you're really
telling me is that I have no choice about staying on.
I'm out of a job, is that it?' Cindy's mind raced
ahead. It wasn't the end of the world. She didn't need
to work at all. She was in the fortunate position of
having a very substantial private income. A few weeks
spent looking around for another job would make not
the slightest difference to her. Except that she'd be
bored—bored stiff. She didn't work for the money. In
fact, she spent more than she took home from Bryant's
on the rent of her luxury flat. Considerably more.

But Sheila was shaking her head and was so busy
shrieking with laughter she could hardly speak. 'Twin-
Set and Pearls? *Her*? You've got to be joking! Can you
just see her and Zac Stone working together? Oh, my
God!'

'Will you calm down, please. If this man's coming
out of retirement, he isn't going to bring a secretary in
with him. And if Twin-Set—if Miss Druce hasn't got
the job, then I've got it. Right? Come on, Sheila, put me
out of my misery!'

Sheila's laughter began to fade. 'Are you telling me
you fancy the idea of working for Zac Stone?'

'I don't know what you mean,' Cindy answered truthfully. 'Why shouldn't I fancy it?'

'After what John's just told you?'

'I make up my own mind about people—you should know that by now. I put up with you from time to time, don't I?'

'Thanks! Listen, seriously——'

'For heaven's sake, am I keeping my job or am I not?'

'Yes, yes. The job's yours ...' Sheila let out an unpleasant snort '... subject to your having a little chat with the man himself.'

'So? That presents no problem. I'm over-qualified for this job as it is.'

'Cocky, aren't you?' Coming from Sheila, that was rather like the pot calling the kettle black. 'Qualifications have little to do with it. Zac will want to know all there is to know about you ...'

'I've got nothing to hide.'

'... including where your birthmarks are and what size bra cup you take.'

Cindy put on her most bored expression, which was very disconcerting to most people. 'Don't be silly.' In truth she was stifling her mirth. Sheila really was funny at times, and Alison had collapsed with laughter. 'Unless you're trying to tell me the man's some kind of lecher?'

'Hardly!' After lighting what must have been her fifth cigarette in the space of an hour, Sheila slithered off the desk, the short skirt riding up her thighs making Cindy flinch inwardly. 'Right, Miss Cool, maybe you'll pass the test. But I'll tell you this for nothing—you won't last two minutes working for Zac Stone.'

It was the first time ever that Sheila had managed actually to needle Cindy. She probably hadn't done it deliberately. It was hard to tell. There was no real malice in the woman. Still, that didn't alter the effect of her words. 'Meaning what?'

Sheila started walking towards the door. 'Meaning

you're too soft for this business. Meaning that you're not made of the right stuff. Meaning that Zac Stone will wipe the floor with a girl like you. You're too . . . nice.' Somehow she managed to make it sound like an insult. Then she added, redeeming herself, 'Honestly, Cindy. And what I really wanted to tell you is that there's a secretarial job coming up shortly at Cookson Associates. I heard it on the grapevine. The secretary to the Creative Director is pregnant, the job'll be up for grabs soon.'

Cindy bowed her head gracefully as Sheila left the room. Then she let out a long, exasperated sigh. 'Won't last two minutes, indeed! Well, we'll see about that!'

Alison looked at her uncertainly. 'She's very blunt, isn't she?'

'Yes,' Cindy agreed. 'Still, at least one knows where one stands with Sheila.'

The two of them looked at one another and giggled. Alison was fresh from secretarial college and had been working as Cindy's assistant for two months. They got on extremely well together. In Alison, Cindy could see herself. When she was nineteen she, too, had been an assistant secretary, though she'd never been as shy as Alison. Still, given a little longer in this business, that would soon be knocked out of her.

Alison was a couple of stones overweight, and very selfconscious about it, which probably accounted for much of her shyness. She was an intelligent, pretty girl with a mop of dark, tightly curled hair, and she thought Cindy was the most super person she'd ever met—next to her aged grandmother. Cindy had rocked with laughter when Alison had gone so far as to tell her that. But she'd been pleased, naturally.

'Listen,' Cindy looked around the office, at the two stark white walls and the two ghastly red ones, 'are you responsible for this? I mean, did you choose this red?'

'No!' Alison looked horrified. 'Actually, I like it, but I knew you'd hate it. I know you like pastel colours. I wasn't even consulted. Mr Stone told the decorators what to do in here and in his own office. I suppose he would have asked you what you wanted, but you weren't here to consult.'

'Mm. Well, thanks for looking after my plants, anyway. I can see at a glance you've done a good job.' Cindy got to her feet and inspected her potted plants, all nine of them, one by one. She adored plants and was very successful with them. Her only regret was that she didn't have a garden to look after these days. But there were no gardens at all surrounding the block where she lived—so she couldn't even sit in one unless she walked to the nearest park. But the flat had its compensations. It was extremely comfortable, probably as safe as one could hope to be in central London, and it was just about within walking distance from Bryant's.

'Aren't you curious to see what Mr Stone's office looks like?'

Cindy's eyes trailed towards the intercommunicating door. 'Very,' she laughed. 'If it's anything like this one, it'll be——' She stopped short as the thought struck her. 'Alison, what time is he coming in? I mean, it's almost ten-thirty.'

'Oh, sorry, I haven't had a chance to tell you. He told me to let you know he won't be in till tomorrow. He said he'd talk to you first thing. He talked to everyone else last week.'

Zac Stone's office could only be described as efficient. Gone was the mahogany desk and the hefty furniture which John had used, which had at least given the room some character. The new desk was white, set in a tubular steel frame. In fact the overall impression of the office was of stainless steel and lightness. The walls were off-white, the three paintings on them steel-framed and wishy-washy. There was a row of filing cabinets in light grey, several spotlights and a couple of glass-topped coffee tables. Around the coffee tables there were four swivel chairs and sitting under the window was a four-seater settee.

'It's—er—functional, I suppose.' Cindy opened the

big cupboards which were built into a recess. The top half of them still housed books and magazines, newspaper clippings and so on. But the bottom half—well, the few bottles of sherry and wine which John had kept there had been added to, and then some. There was every sort of spirit you could think of, various mixers, a crate of vintage wine, an ice bucket and assorted glasses.

'Look at this lot, Alison. Obviously Mr Stone believes in keeping the clients well entertained!' She turned from the cupboard to find her assistant looking at her rather wistfully.

'That's a gorgeous dress, Cindy. I wish I could wear those strappy little numbers. I wish I had a figure like yours! I just don't seem to be losing any weight at all.'

'Don't worry about it,' Cindy soothed, knowing only too well how the younger girl felt. 'I've told you, from the age of ten to the age of sixteen, I was overweight. Very. It's only puppy fat. It'll go in its own good time.'

'But I'm so much shorter than you!' Alison groaned. 'It's very hard to believe you were ever overweight. Are you sure you're not just saying that to make me feel better?'

'Honestly,' Cindy assured her, 'I was. I'll dig out an old photograph and show you. Are you keeping up with that diet I gave you before I went away? The health foods?'

Alison pulled a face. 'Yes. Well, I don't care much for health foods. I—I have slipped once or twice.'

'That,' Cindy said firmly, 'is entirely up to you. Nobody can do it for you.'

Cindy did some of her own shopping at the health food shop. While she was not obsessive about food, she was particular about what she ate. She believed in the old adage that you are what you eat, and if her skin was anything to go by then a varied and well-balanced diet really did pay dividends. Her skin was as flawless as her figure.

She had become body-conscious at an early age, while she was attending the exclusive boarding school her parents had picked out for her at birth. The mocking cruelty of her contemporaries had left their mark and from the age of sixteen onwards, when the excess weight finally started to melt away, Cindy had kept a very careful watch on her figure. Never again did she want to have clothes specially made for her because she was an odd shape.

These days, she had to admit to being very indulgent as far as clothes were concerned. She loved them, and thanks to the money her grandmother had left her, she could afford to buy what she wanted. Cindy was not a follower of fashion, nor did she like clothes which she regarded as fussy. She wore what suited her and had often been complimented on her clothes sense. Especially by James.

Damn him.

At noon Cindy escaped from Bryant's and spent a quiet half hour sitting on a bench on the tiny green patch in Hanover Square. All morning she had been accosted by one member or another of the agency's staff. Gossip was rife. The grapevine was working overtime. The atmosphere at work was one of awe mingled with excitement and, in some quarters, apprehension.

When she spotted Miss Druce walking towards her, Cindy felt trapped. She couldn't just get up and walk away, because Twin-Set and Pearls—as Sheila called her—was waving vigorously.

'Good morning, Cindy.' Miss Druce lowered herself on to the bench rather tiredly. She was a middle-aged woman who had worked for Mr Bryant for almost twenty years, and if anyone was ill-suited to the world of advertising, it was she. At least, she was these days. Like the retired Chairman, Miss Druce had never kept up with the times. In fact Sheila's label of 'Twin-Set and Pearls' described Miss Druce in a nutshell. Sheila's nicknames were always spot-on.

'Did you have a nice holiday?'

'Quite pleasant, thank you,' said Cindy, somewhat evasively.

Miss Druce eyed the bare skin of Cindy's shoulders and the skimpy sun-dress with a hint of disapproval in her eyes. 'We've been very lucky with the weather lately, haven't we? You got a nice suntan, I must say.'

'Thank you.' Feeling slightly ill at ease, Cindy smiled politely. She could see what was coming. 'I spent most of my time in the garden.'

'You were visiting your parents in Cheshire, of course. How is Sir Robert?'

'He's fine, thank you.' Miss Druce spoke of Cindy's father as if she knew him, which she didn't.

'And your mother?'

'Very well. Everybody was fine, thanks.'

And then it came, but there was no hint of the sour grapes Cindy had anticipated. 'So, starting tomorrow you'll be working as secretary to Mr Stone?' There was a liveliness about Miss Druce's eyes Cindy had never seen before.

'Yes, so it seems.' She looked at the older woman curiously. 'And you're staying on at Bryant's, too.'

'Yes, of course.' Miss Druce gave a satisfied nod. 'I discussed the matter very thoroughly with Mr Stone, naturally. Cindy, let me tell you, he's a charming man! Absolutely charming! You and he will get on splendidly, I know it.'

By now, Cindy had heard such varying reports about Zac Stone that she took nothing as real. She was determined to remain neutral, unaffected by any sort of gossip. 'One hopes so.'

'Of course, I could have taken the job myself,' Miss Druce went on. 'But after discussing things with Mr Stone, I thought no, he really wants someone a little more . . . dynamic.' She gave a little laugh.

Cindy laughed, too. 'That's hardly a word I'd use to describe myself, Miss Druce.'

'Perhaps, perhaps. However, as you know, I'd had things rather easy lately, working for Mr Bryant. I mean, I've been virtually a part-timer and rather spoiled. In fact, Mr Stone asked me whether I'd rather stay on and just work part time officially. But I said no. Firstly, frankly, I need full-time money and secondly—well, we'd all rather be busy, wouldn't we? It's so bad for the character, not having enough to do with one's time. Anyway, Mr Stone suggested I might like to supervise the typing pool. There are six girls there, as you know, and I thought it a very good idea.'

As Cindy opened her mouth to make a tactful comment, Miss Druce rushed on, 'Mr Stone said that my experience and expertise could be passed on to the younger girls. He's quite a perfectionist, I believe, as I am, of course. So I agreed to take the task on, and I must say that from what I've seen so far, those girls certainly need supervising . . .'

Miss Druce went on and on. And on. The latter half of Cindy's lunch-hour was far from restful.

When she walked into the sanctuary of her flat that evening, Cindy felt exhausted. Yet she'd done nothing all day. There had been no work to do. The ear-bashing she'd taken from Miss Druce and umpteen other people had tired her out. Of course it was all a nine-day wonder. Within a couple of weeks everything and everyone at Bryant's would settle down into a routine, albeit a different one.

She was soaking in the bath when the telephone rang. All thoughts of Bryant's and everyone connected with the place had vanished. She was mulling over the two weeks she had spent with her family. It had been nice being in the country again, spending time in the gardens, doing some riding. But it had been very much a duty visit, a once-yearly duty visit. She'd done it, as she always did, for her mother's sake. And only for her mother's sake.

It was James on the telephone.

Good manners, and nothing else, prevented her from putting the receiver down. 'What do you want, James?'

'Aw, Cindy, don't be like that! Please!' The voice was half-jocular, coaxing.

'This is pointless. Look, what we had together is

over. Finished. Everything our relationship stood for was negated, dissolved—by you, James. Goodbye.'

'Cindy! I *must* talk to you. You don't understand!'

'There's no point,' Cindy said tiredly, 'you're a hypocrite. You'd better face that fact.' She wasn't angry with James. She never had been angry with him. Just disappointed. *Disappointed.* But she shouldn't have been. She should have known better than to put her trust in someone. After all, how many people were faithful these days?

'Please hear me out.' James' voice was serious now. 'I've been in agony this past couple of weeks, waiting for you to get back from Cheshire. May I come over and talk to you?'

'Absolutely not.'

There was a pause. 'Are you telling me it's over?'

'I told you that before I went away, and again two minutes ago.' Cindy promptly replaced the receiver. There was no point in continuing the conversation.

Pulling her bath towel closer around her, she went into the lounge, taking solace and pleasure from the order and décor of the room. She had her flat just as she wanted it and it was good, so good to be in the quiet and privacy of her own place.

Financially, she was a very lucky girl. She appreciated that. On the face of things, Cindy was a girl who had everything. But that was far from the truth. She lived with the feeling that life was passing her by. Deep inside her there was a discontentment which sometimes kept her awake at nights. If she could only put a name to it, she might be able to do something about it.

She sat on the settee and put her feet up, eyes closing. Life was so . . . so bland. It was neither boring nor exciting. It was just an unfolding of days. She wished she'd gone abroad for a couple of weeks instead of visiting her family. Perhaps a complete change would have lifted this mild depression she couldn't seem to shake off. Of course, the James thing hadn't helped. She was coming to the conclusion that she was no good with people. Perhaps she should stick to plants. They seemed to be the only thing in life she really succeeded——

The sound of a high-powered drill brought her eyes open. She groaned loudly. Since getting back from Cheshire on Saturday she had been subjected to the intermittent drilling and banging from next door. The adjoining flat had stood empty for the past five weeks, but it was clearly being altered or prepared for a new tenant. Fine. But did they have to work during the evening as well as during the weekend?

She closed her eyes again and tried to blot out the grating noise. It was impossible. Sighing, Cindy glanced towards the clock. It wasn't even eight yet, and the long summer evening stretched ahead of her. But it would be too much effort to get dressed and go for a walk in the park.

There seemed little else to do but take an early night.

CHAPTER TWO

'GOOD morning, Cindy.' Alison lowered her voice and jerked a thumb towards the adjoining door. 'He's in! He buzzed through about ten minutes ago and——'

Cindy started laughing. 'Speak up, Alison! He can't hear you through a closed door, can he?'

Unconvinced, Alison continued in a whisper. 'He buzzed ·through about ten minutes ago and said you should go in to see him when you arrived.'

'Fine. I'll just pop to the loo first.' Cindy dropped her lightweight jacket over the back of her chair. She was sorry she'd worn it, even if it did match her dress, because she hadn't needed it. It was a glorious morning, warm already, and the walk to the office had lifted her spirits.

'Don't be nervous. I've told you, Mr Stone's a very nice man.'

With a new bout of laughter tinkling on the air, Cindy did her own bit of reassuring in return. 'I'm not nervous, silly. I just want to comb my hair!'

The dress looked good with the suntan. It was white, close-fitting in the bodice, with two thin shoulder-straps, and straight in the skirt. Cindy smoothed it down and ran a comb through her shoulder-length hair, a little impatient with the curls which no amount of blow-drying would straighten out completely. It was naturally blonde, and her recent spell in the sun had added to its highlights.

She didn't bother with eye-shadow during the day, just a touch of mascara, which was all her dark eyes needed really, and lipstick. After freshening her lipstick she stood back and gave a satisfied nod at her full-length reflection. She was presentable.

26

After a second's hesitation at the door of her office, Cindy smiled to herself and walked on. She would enter Mr Stone's office via the door which led to the corridor. Alison would think she'd been waylaid by someone when she didn't return, and that would stop her worrying over Cindy being nervous while meeting her new boss!

'Come!'

The voice responded to the knock and Cindy responded to the voice.

Zac Stone was bent over a pad on his desk, scribbling away. It was seconds before the head of jet black hair was raised and deep blue eyes, very deep blue eyes, met Cindy's gaze.

She stood, with the sun streaming in from the windows now almost directly behind her, erect and elegant, with her head tilted just slightly to one side. It was something she always did, unconsciously, when she was either listening intently or intrigued by what she saw.

She was intrigued by what she saw.

He was wearing a crisp, pale blue shirt of the finest cotton. Through it Cindy could see the shadow of dark hair covering his chest. The top button of the shirt was open and his tie, still knotted, had been loosened, dragged carelessly to one side. His shirt sleeves were rolled up, and the depth of the tan on his forearms made Cindy look pale by comparison. On his wrist there was a gold watch; it was neat, not ostentatious, just wildly expensive.

Zac Stone's eyes seemed to be looking deep inside her. He was unsmiling but not uninterested and Cindy felt, Cindy knew, that he had taken in the details of her appearance as thoroughly as she had absorbed the details of his.

Seeing him had come as a shock to her and she mentally told herself off for it, for the brief flutter of . . . *was* it nervousness? . . . that was making her stomach contract slightly.

His face was—would handsome be the right word? It was certainly an attractive face, with strong, clear-cut features, a straight nose and . . . Suddenly, Cindy could hear her grandmother's voice as clearly as if the old lady were standing next to her . . . 'Dimple on chin, devil within.'

Without realising it she smiled.

Zac Stone's eyebrows rose almost imperceptibly. The few seconds' surveillance was over, shattered with the silence when he spoke. 'Good morning. I don't believe we've met. I'm Zac Stone, and you are . . .?'

There was nothing in his voice, no accent to indicate that he was Welsh. He had an attractive voice in that it was deep, with an unusual timbre. It was almost . . . almost gravelly.

He had got to his feet as he spoke, but he didn't proffer his hand. He was a big man, lean but broad, and despite the added stature given to Cindy by her high-heeled sandals his height was superior by a good six inches.

'Miss Hetherington, Cindy Hetherington.' She made no attempt to sit down. It was polite to wait until you were asked, wasn't it?

Mr Stone's eyes left hers and flitted briefly towards the intercommunicating door, a slight frown appearing between his brows, and when the eyes came back to Cindy's, his frown deepened. 'You are Cindy Hetherington?'

The emphasis on the first word made Cindy wonder whether he was disappointed—or what. Maybe he'd been expecting someone older, someone more like Miss Druce? Or was it simply that he hadn't expected her to come in through the other door?

'Well. Sit down, Cindy, sit down.' The frown cleared as he waved her towards the chair facing his desk.

As Cindy moved forward he watched her, blatantly, his eyes moving slowly from the top of her head, over the details of her face and down the length of her slender figure. But the deep blue eyes were unreadable and the set of his mouth, still unsmiling, left her guessing as to what was in his thoughts. She knew only that she didn't feel quite as confident in herself as she had when she'd entered this room. But Zac Stone couldn't know that. Nor would he. Sheila hadn't labelled her Miss Cool for nothing.

'It's nice to meet you, Mr Stone.' Cindy spoke up first, meeting his eyes levelly. Her soft, well modulated voice was clear and steady, revealing nothing but a polite neutrality. 'As you're no doubt aware, I was away on holiday for the past two weeks, so I learned the news of Bryant's takeover only yesterday.'

There was a slight hesitation before he responded. 'And how did you feel about it?'

She, too, hesitated before she replied. She had to think about that one. 'Interested.'

'You want to stay on, I take it?'

'Yes.'

'How long have you worked in advertising?'

'Four years.' She suspected from the wording of his question that he wanted to discover whether his name was known to her. It was that, rather than an enquiry as to her experience, which would come later.

Mr Stone's next question proved her right. 'So you're aware that I sold my original agency two years ago, that I've been off the advertising scene since then and living abroad?'

'Of course.'

'Of course.' He smiled slightly.

'Well, the transaction was reported in *Campaign* and even so, the inter-agency grapevine is very efficient, as I'm sure you're well aware.' Cindy shrugged her slender shoulders, crossing one leg over another as she spoke. 'I want the job as your secretary, Mr Stone, and if you're asking whether I'm aware of your reputation, the answer is yes. It precedes you wherever you go.'

'I wasn't.' The answer came quickly, and the blue eyes flashed at her. There was a hard edge to his voice, letting her know she'd spoken out of turn. 'And I'm well aware of that, too.'

Cindy was unperturbed. In her opinion there was nothing wrong with what she'd said.

Zac Stone looked down at an empty space on his desk, resting his big frame against his chair in the momentary silence. It was as if he were clearing his mind of something. When next he spoke the edge had gone from his voice. 'How long did you work for John Daws, Cindy?'

'Two years. This is the only agency I've worked in. I started here when I was nineteen as an assistant secretary to the Creative Director. I was in that job for six months, then I worked as secretary to the Financial Director for a year. After that I spent six months with an Account Director and then, because I'd had all-round experience, the M.D. asked me to work for him. I was with him until he—left—two weeks ago.'

Mr Stone nodded briefly. 'Good. So, tell me something about yourself.'

The question came as a surprise and she looked at him quickly, not quite understanding. 'I thought I just did.'

'I meant tell me something about yourself, not about your career.'

'Oh! Well, I'm—er—I come from Cheshire, which is where I was born. I'm unmarried, almost twenty-four, interested in gardening, philosophy, yoga, psychology . . .' Her voice trailed off; he looked positively bored. 'Perhaps you'd like to be more specific, Mr Stone?'

Deliberately, insolently, Zac Stone's eyes moved down the length of her body, coming to rest on her bare, beautifully tanned legs. 'What do you do with your evenings?'

She was thrown completely now, and the first hint of annoyance gripped her. 'I'm sorry,' she said quietly, and as nonchalantly as she could manage, 'but I don't see the relevance of that question.'

'The relevance to what?'

'To my working as your secretary.'

'Don't you?' The edge was back in the deep voice. 'I suggest you answer it just the same. I suggest also that you try being a little more co-operative—if you're sure you want this job.'

If she's sure she wants the job? Cindy shifted slightly in her seat. She did want the job. She'd also taken it for granted she had already got the job, but Zac Stone obviously hadn't! Things were not turning out as she had expected. This was no informal chat by way of introducing themselves, this was an interview!

A flash of indignation rushed through her. Good grief, she could *eat* this job—and before this interview was over she'd make certain Zac Stone realised that!

She didn't care for the way his eyes had raked over her. And she still didn't see the relevance of his question, but she hadn't meant to appear unco-operative. 'I go to the theatre once or twice a week. When evening classes are in session, I go there. Of course there aren't any during the summer. I dine out quite often. I sometimes take my car and go for a drive. Fridays, I sometimes pop down to the coast and spend the weekend by the sea. You know, the usual sort of things.'

'Those are "the usual" sort of things, are they?' The sarcasm in his voice was unmistakable.

Their eyes met and held for a long moment. There seemed to be a total lack of communication between them. They seemed to be at cross purposes.

As if he were making an effort to be patient with her, Mr Stone asked, 'How much do we pay you?'

When Cindy answered that one, he nodded, as if he'd known the answer all along. 'It's not exactly a fortune, is it?'

Cindy smiled, her elegant hands making a sweeping gesture in the air. 'The so-called glamorous jobs are often poorly paid.'

'And where do you live? Do you have far to commute?'

'No. I'm lucky enough to live in walking distance, actually—well, just about. I live off Belgrave Square.'

'A very expensive place to live.' Zac Stone nodded curtly. He drew in a long, slow breath, watching her carefully as he spoke. 'So, you live in one of the most costly areas of London, your spare time entertainment is . . . shall we say extravagant? . . . and from the look of things, you buy your shoes and handbags in Bond Street. Am I to assume from all this that you've got yourself a sugar-daddy?'

Cindy almost lost her composure. His remark, his assumption, his *audacity* was so unexpected that she started in surprise. Without pausing to think, she put him right swiftly, her voice tremulous with indignation. 'No, Mr Stone! You're to assume no such thing!'

'A rich boy-friend, then?'

Now it wasn't his words which infuriated her so much as the laughter which flitted across the watchful, deep blue eyes. The nerve of the man! Was he goading her deliberately? 'Wrong again. I haven't got a boy-friend at all!'

Cindy's hands tightened on the handbag which was resting on her lap. She let her eyes drift towards the window, let the awkward silence hang between herself and the wretched man who was interviewing her. She didn't have to take this! She could get up, right now, and just walk out of this place.

But the penny suddenly dropped and Cindy's indignation dissipated as she realised how odd her answers must have sounded to someone who didn't know anything about her. And Zac Stone didn't know anything about her, anything at all! How could he, why should he? To all intents and purposes Cindy was an ordinary working girl who was being interviewed for a secretarial job. What she took for granted, her private income, her lifestyle—well, perhaps she couldn't really blame him for jumping to all sorts of conclusions.

Or could she? Why did he assume she had a sugar-daddy in tow? She knew full well that there was nothing about her which might give a person the impression she was the sort of girl who would . . . Damn Zac Stone! He'd goaded her deliberately. She had no evidence of it; she just knew it! What the devil was he up to?

But when Cindy turned to look at him again, she ended up giving him the benefit of the doubt. He was looking at her expectantly, almost innocently. She just couldn't weigh him up. But then, surely, that was the problem between them. He'd been unable to weigh her up.

'Mr Stone, I have a private income, but it obviously never occured to me that I should start this interview by telling you that.'

'That's perfectly reasonable,' he shrugged. 'Any more than I would have started the interview by asking you if your salary were supplemented in some way.'

'Perhaps we'd better start again?'

'I think so.' He smiled at her. It was a genuine smile, and a very attractive one at that. Cindy relaxed again . . . and yet—and yet in the corner of her mind there was a doubt. About him. She'd been put on her guard; she didn't trust him. But damn it all, she was more than intrigued by him!

Mr Stone flicked a switch on the intercom on his desk. It was a moment before Alison answered. 'Yes, Mr Stone?'

'Alison, would you make two cups of coffee, please. Cindy's in here with me.'

'Oh! I thought—er—yes, right away, Mr Stone.'

Cindy suppressed a smile. At Alison's surprise—and at the near reverence in her voice.

After switching off the intercom he then picked up the internal telephone and punched out two numbers. 'Is that Bill—no, it's John, isn't it? Would you bring me the personnel file on Cindy Hetherington? Right away, please, John.'

Well, Mr Stone seemed to talk to his staff nicely enough. John Crosdale would be bringing the file. John, who'd presumed Zac Stone to have been born out of wedlock! The personnel files were kept in John's department, accounts, because Bryant's didn't have a personnel department as such.

As far as Cindy was concerned the interview was taking a turn for the better. Mr Stone would see for himself, when he looked at her personnel file, just how well qualified she was. She settled back comfortably in her seat, her confidence and composure now fully restored. It would be a challenge, working for a man like Zac Stone. And that, a job she could really get her teeth into, was just what she needed to fill her life.

'Right. While we're waiting for the file let me fill you in on one or two things.' Mr Stone's voice was crisp and businesslike. 'Since you didn't see the relevance of my earlier question, I will explain it to you. Had I learned that you were on the verge of marriage, pregnancy or some similar commitment, there'd have been no point in our continuing this interview. The same applies if you are committed to someone, or something, which necessitates your leaving the office on the dot of five each evening. I take it you are not?'

'No. I'm quite free.'

'If you work for me, you'll work longer hours than those you worked for John Daws, and that does not automatically entitle you to a raise in salary.' In a tone that seemed slightly disparaging, he added, 'In the circumstances, that clearly won't bother you too much.'

Cindy said nothing, she was too busy trying to decide whether he was putting her down in some way. Was it just her imagination, or did he seem to resent her independence?

'I start work at eight-thirty,' he went on. 'And I finish when I've finished for the day. Where I go, my secretary goes. When I'm on these premises, she'll be in the next room. When I'm out seeing clients, she'll be by my side. Understood?'

'Understood.'

'Have you got a current passport?'

'Of course.'

'But of course.' There it was again, that hint of sarcasm. 'You'd have to be prepared for all contingencies. To work over the weekend, if I deem it necessary. Or to work halfway through the night.'

Cindy was beginning to see what John Crosdale had meant. 'Professional', Sheila had said. My, my, what a mild word, coming from Sheila! Cindy smiled inwardly at her own thoughts. She was almost enjoying herself now. With his sarcasm and his threats that she might have to work all the hours God sends, Zac Stone was trying to put her off the job.

'Do you still want to work for me?'

'But of course.' She said it sweetly, knowing full well that her smile would not take the sting from her choice of words. Two could play at that game.

It surprised her that his only reaction was a slight pull at the corners of his lips. Her eyes lingered there, on the firmness of his mouth. At first glance she would have described him as thin-lipped, but there was a curve, a sensuality about the lower lip which spoke of . . . 'I'm sorry, what did you say?' Shocked at herself, at the way her mind had wandered, Cindy looked at him blankly, wide-eyed. She hadn't heard a word.

'I said, what the hell is it with you, Cindy? What's a girl like you doing in a place like this? You are, are you not, the daughter of Sir Robert Hetherington?'

Before she had chance to reply, there was a knock on the door and John Crosdale walked in with Cindy's personnel file under his arm. He bade her good morning, but she didn't even hear him. She was looking at Zac Stone in astonishment. So he knew who her father was. Well, it wasn't all that surprising. Her father's name had been in the newspapers more than once, although not very recently. But Zac Stone had put two and two together and made four. More to the point, *when* had he realised who her father was?

John walked around the desk and placed the file in front of the new M.D. and, glancing meaningfully at the file and then at Cindy, he shrugged exaggeratedly,

pulling a face as he did so. It was designed to let Cindy
know that this was unusual, that in last week's 'chats'
with the rest of the staff, Zac Stone hadn't bothered to
go through anyone else's personal file.

Cindy met John's eyes and nodded.

'Thank you, John.' Ostensibly, it was a dismissal, but
Zac said it in such a way that both Cindy and John
were left with the feeling that he must have eyes in the
back of his head. He'd caught the message John had
intended for Cindy. He didn't miss a thing!

'Zac.' With his eyes rolling upwards, John left the
room.

'I am Robert Hetherington's daughter, yes. Have you
. . . have you met my father?' The chances of that were
slim, but it was the only solution Cindy could think of.

Zac didn't answer. He flipped open the file, took a
cursory glance at the first page, an even quicker glance
at the second page and then unclipped Cindy's
curriculum vitae from the rest of the papers.

Cindy had submitted the CV with her application for
a job at Bryant's four years ago. It comprised three
sheets of paper and gave a brief outline of her life; her
education, qualifications, and so on. Zac Stone eyed
each sheet briefly, then let it fall to the desk.

'No,' he turned his attention back to Cindy, 'I
haven't met your father. I read a comprehensive article
about him in the newspaper when he retired as a
Queen's Counsel.'

Cindy frowned. 'That was eighteen months ago.'

Zac smiled. 'I have a photographic memory.'

More sarcasm.

She still couldn't make head nor tail of the man.
'How did you make the connection? It couldn't have
been just the name . . .'

'It was that and the fact that you come from
Cheshire. There can't be many extremely wealthy
families in Cheshire with the name of Hetherington.'

'But . . .' Cindy was growing quite confused. If he'd
made the connection, and he knew of her family's

wealth, why had he said what he'd said about a sugar-daddy?

He watched her, waiting until she'd formed the question in her mind, then pre-empted her. 'I couldn't be sure it was Daddy who was keeping you in the lap of luxury, could I?'

She didn't put him right. It wasn't her father's money but a bequest from her grandmother that Cindy lived on. The thought of her accepting a penny from her father was laughable. Nor did she contradict him about living in the lap of luxury, even though it was a gross exaggeration. Cindy held her tongue because she was in danger of spoiling things. If she told Zac Stone her impressions of him, she'd talk herself right out of a job. And it was rapidly becoming a matter of principle to her that she landed this job.

Inwardly, however, she was fuming. And she got even more cross when he repeated what he had asked her just before John interrupted them. 'So what is it with you, Cynthia? Why are you bothering to work at all?'

Her given name grated on her ears, especially the way he'd used it. 'Everybody calls me Cindy, if you don't mind. I much prefer it.'

'I can understand that,' he said drily. He tapped the papers on his desk. 'There's a year unaccounted for here. What were you doing between the age of eighteen and nineteen?'

'Nothing. I——'

'Nothing? Then why work now? Judging from the status of your family, your history, you've had everything handed to you on a silver platter. What makes you think you could hold down a job with me? What makes you think you've got what it takes? How the hell did you get into this world in the first place? Is Sam Bryant your uncle or something?'

The sound of Cindy's breath catching in her throat was made inaudible by the knock on the adjoining door. Alison walked in with a tray of coffee and placed it carefully on the desk. Cindy could feel the heat of her anger rising to her cheeks. She was so cross she couldn't have spoken if she'd wanted to. Who the hell did Zac Stone think he was? How dared he speak to her like that? He was putting her down because she just happened to be born into a wealthy family! And no one had done that before, not even Sheila.

As Cindy's eyes flitted towards Alison she saw that the youngster's eyes had widened in alarm. Alison was busying herself with the coffee, adding milk and just a few grains of brown sugar for Cindy. She'd seen the file on the boss's desk and, no doubt, the two pink patches that had appeared in Cindy's cheeks. Cindy wasn't coping!

Cindy had the dreadful feeling she was letting Alison down. It wouldn't have occurred to Alison that Cindy might not get this job. It hadn't occurred to Cindy that she mightn't get the job! Well, she'd be damned if she didn't! What had Sheila said? Something about passing a test . . . *Was* this a test, and if so, had everyone had to endure it?

But of course they had! She must be getting paranoid, thinking Mr Stone was picking only on her. A man like him, he would want to know what motivated his staff, what made them tick. 'He'll want to know all there is to know about you . . .'

She looked at Zac Stone through new eyes then. He was rich, he was successful, he was powerful. Those who couldn't stand his pace had been fired or had left of their own accord. And Sheila had warned her that she wouldn't last two minutes. She would prove Sheila wrong. She would prove Zac Stone wrong in whatever he was assuming her to be. And quite apart from that, she would prove to herself that she could get this job, and hold it down.

And she would do it with dignity.

Fortunately, Alison was relating to Mr Stone a message she had just taken over the phone. It gave Cindy precious minutes in which to think. He had no good reason for refusing her the job—provided she could show him that she had what it took. Provided she could pass his test. He'd been trying to frighten her off. He'd been goading her, and she'd risen to the bait. But that was all finished now. She wouldn't rise to it again—ever!

When Alison left, with a frantic glance in her direction, Cindy settled back comfortably in her chair and picked up her coffee cup. She laughed softly, 'No, Mr Bryant isn't my uncle. I was employed here entirely on my own merits. Anyway, to answer your questions— I'm working because I have a lively mind which enjoys being stimulated. And I'd be bored stiff sitting at home twiddling my thumbs all day. I don't *think* I've got what it takes to work for you, I know I have. I'll be perfectly happy to work long hours, if that's what you want, and I'll hold the job down because apart from being well qualified as a secretary I'm also well versed in all aspects of agency work, and I've got a good deal of common sense.'

Cindy was talking coolly, clearly, and she didn't pause to let him get a word in. 'I chose advertising because the psychology behind it fascinates me. I'm interested in what motivates people to buy things. I'm interested in what motivates people to do all sorts of things. I don't think of this as a glamorous job; I think I'm in a tough, competitive world where only the strong and the shrewd survive.'

She looked at him levelly, and waited. When Zac Stone remained silent, she, too, said nothing more. But her eyes were watching his over the rim of her cup. She would have given a lot to know what was going through his mind, but Zac's face remained impassive. This was make or break, she was aware of that. She was also a little nervous of all the claims she'd made, hoping that she would indeed be able to live up to them—if she were given the chance.

He grunted. He was assessing, considering, weighing. Then he picked up his cup and said nothing till he'd finished his coffee. 'Tell me, did you once consider modelling as a career? I see you took a modelling course when you were younger.'

Cindy was taken aback. He'd glanced at the papers on her file so quickly she didn't think he'd had chance to register everything. 'No, never. I took that course because it polishes one off as far as poise and deportment are concerned. Mummy wasn't quite satisfied with the way they'd turned me out of finishing school, and the course also taught things like make-up, hair care, manicure and so on.'

Inwardly, Cindy was smiling because at the time she had taken the course she was still a little overweight. She had been totally lacking in dress sense and without the first clue as to what she wanted to do with her life. She had been floating, and she suspected her mother had sent her on the course mainly to give her something to do. But it had, in fact, done a great deal for Cindy. 'Of course,' she added, thinking aloud, 'Mummy would never have dreamt of steering me towards modelling as a career!'

When Zac threw her a filthy look, she had no idea what she'd said wrong. If he'd known her when she was seventeen he'd have seen the point in her remark! 'Is there anything else I can tell you about myself?' she asked lightly.

'Yes.' He sounded positively annoyed. 'I see you concentrated on languages during the latter part of your education, then you spent a year with friends of your family in the South of France. Just how good is your French?'

Cindy's eyes widened. He hadn't been joking about his memory. He recalled every word on the papers he'd glanced at. 'Almost as good as my English.'

'And your German?'

'Not so good. Enough to get by, though.'

'You'd use your shorthand very little with me. I prefer to talk to a machine.'

'That's fine. I'm quite at home with a dictaphone.' He had no good reason for refusing her the job, and he knew it.

He shrugged, open the top drawer of his desk and flung a cassette in Cindy's direction. 'Start with this,' he said curtly. 'Alison will tell you how I like letters set out. She did a letter for me last week—three times. I trust you'll do better.' He picked up the personnel file, shoved the papers back into it and handed it to her. 'Take that back to John Crosdale. Then pick up some petty cash and go out and buy a decent coffee set— something modern. Throw this flowery stuff away. Buzz Sheila and tell her I want her in my office, together with everyone else who works on the Simpson account, at eleven-thirty on the dot. Then phone Simpson's and arrange a meeting with them at their offices one day next week—any time that Mr Simpson himself can be present. Then type a memo to the departmental heads and say there's to be a meeting in the conference room at three on Thursday afternoon . . . Well, what are you waiting for?'

Cindy's sense of victory was mild, very mild. There was—it was unmistakable now—a nervousness clutching at her stomach. But there was no way she would let its how. To him, or to anyone else. Calmly she gathered up the coffee cups, put the file on the tray and the cassette on the file. 'Yes, Mr Stone.'

As she moved towards the adjoining door, she could feel Zac Stone's eyes boring into her. 'And Cindy,' he said crisply, almost reluctantly, 'you'd better make it Zac from now on.'

She turned and smiled. 'Well, thank you—Zac.'

'Don't thank me yet,' he warned. 'You're on trial. We'll give it a month, then talk again. That is, if you're still here by then.'

Cindy said nothing. She'd be there, all right. She'd show him! Immediately the door was closed behind her she put down the tray, held up a silencing hand at Alison and wrote down Zac's instructions. If Alison distracted her she'd be sure to forget at least one of them.

'So you're staying?' Alison whispered as soon as Cindy's hand went down.

'Of course I'm staying. I told you I would.'

'Yes, but—Oh, I'm so glad, Cindy! I'd hate it if I wasn't working with you. Well, what did you think of him?' Alison was jerking her thumb towards the door again. 'Sexy, isn't he? Don't you think he's just gorgeous?'

Cindy couldn't suppress her smile. 'Gorgeous?' she mused. After what she'd just been through? She felt as though she'd been shoved through a wringing machine. 'He struck me as being a little—er—stern.'

'Oh, I don't mean that. You know I didn't mean that!' Alison almost gave it full voice. 'I mean his looks. Don't you think he's just gorgeous looking? Come on, Cindy!'

'He's . . . well, I suppose he's attractive. Sort of.' That was as much as she was prepared to admit. She picked up the internal telephone.

'I wonder what he thought of you?' Alison queried.

But Cindy didn't want to think about the answer to that one.

CHAPTER THREE

CINDY was really thrown in at the deep end. Somehow, she coped. She did that because she was determined. Still, before the day was over she made her first mistake. It wasn't serious, it just infuriated her.

There were nine letters on the tape Zac had given her and she had put them on his desk, beautifully typed, by four o'clock. He emerged from his office at a little before seven and handed her the letter-folder. Get these off tonight, would you?'

Cindy took the folder from him and flipped it open, keeping her voice light and casual as she asked him whether they were calling it a day. He was wearing his jacket and had switched off the light in his office.

'I'm calling it a day,' he said gruffly, 'but you're not.'

'You haven't signed these . . .'

'You haven't set them out properly.' The satisfaction in his voice sickened her. 'I like everything set against the margin, no punctuation in the address—it saves time. Retype them and sign them on my behalf.'

'Sorry.' It was all Cindy could manage to say. She was fuming. With herself, mostly, but at his attitude, too.

'Goodnight,' he drawled then. 'Give the cleaners my regards.'

She glared after him. The office cleaners came in at six in the morning, as he was no doubt well aware. In her anxiety to get through everything he'd given her to do that day, she'd clean forgotten to ask Alison about the setting out of his letters. She retyped them, though it took her far longer than it should have; she was so cross with herself that her typing went awry. It was very late when she got home.

The next day, she saw two different facets of her

43

boss's personality. She saw him being flippant and she saw him being charming.

'Now there's interesting for you!' He spoke to her in a sing-song accent which was exaggeratedly Welsh when he called her into his office during the middle of the morning.

When Cindy looked non-plussed he dropped the accent and explained, still obviously delighted about something, 'I've just had a call from the Ad Manager at Barrats. He invited himself to lunch.'

'Barrats?' Cindy stood, looking cool and crisp in a pink shirtwaister. 'But they're not one of our clients. They do business with Cookson Associates . . .' She caught the twinkle in his eyes. 'I see. So business is coming to you, is it?'

'We'll have to see. We'll be leaving at one.'

'We?'

'Of course, we.' As she nodded, he added, 'Just be sweet to him, don't drink too much wine, and listen to everything he says.'

Cindy did exactly as he'd told her during the two and a half hour luncheon—and Zac said later she'd made a good 'table decoration'. There was no charm for Cindy. Not ever. It was reserved only for the clients.

On Thursday Zac addressed the heads of department and told them about certain changes which would take place in the agency. Towards the end of the meeting he brought up the subject of time-keeping. 'I'm not a clock-watcher. I want a relaxed atmosphere at Bryant's. You can come and go as you please—within reason.' He added that with a look in Sheila's direction. 'All I'm interested in is that the work gets done. When you do it is entirely up to yourselves.'

That did not, of course, apply to Cindy. She got to work at eight-thirty on the dot and didn't leave the office until her boss left the office. Nor was the bit about a relaxed atmosphere applicable to her—Zac saw to that. He taxed her to her limits. He answered her questions, but he gave her not the slightest word of encouragement, or praise. Nor did he speak to her the way he spoke to everyone else. His sarcasm punctuated the day at regular intervals.

But he didn't get a rise out of her. She would not give him best. She never answered him back and she never let him guess what was going through her mind. But there were compensations for her. The job itself had already removed her depression. She was engrossed and fascinated by it even before the week was out.

She was also fascinated by Zac Stone, in spite of disliking the man. He drove himself hard, and Cindy wondered why. Why had he come out of retirement? What was the real man like? Not the Managing Director of Bryant's, not the man who was determined to make her life hell—but the real Zac Stone?

By the end of Cindy's second week she was really beginning to feel the strain. She was working hard, but it wasn't the strain of hard work so much as the strain between herself and Zac. He hadn't been joking when he'd said she'd be on trial.

On the Friday night, when she finally got through the front door of her flat, Cindy sank into the nearest chair and kicked off her shoes, letting her toes curl into the thick pile of the living room carpet. She didn't know which she wanted most, a cup of tea or a hot bath. She amended that to a cool bath; the weather was so sultry at the moment that even the walk home had exhausted her. Her feet were throbbing.

They had finished work around nine tonight, but at least there was no question of going into the office over the weekend. Boy, did she intend to make the most of the weekend! She would lie in tomorrow. She would stay in bed until she woke up naturally, until she'd had as much sleep as she needed! Even the thought of it was luxurious.

It was an effort to go and brew up. She leaned against the kitchen wall as she waited for the kettle to boil, her hand automatically reaching out to pluck two

dying flowers from the geranium on her kitchen
windowsill. Pulling a face, she ran a finger over one of
the slats of the Venetian blinds as she closed them. They
needed washing, but it was just too bad. They'd have to
wait until she could face the task. On Sunday, perhaps.
Maybe by then she would have enough energy to catch
up with her household chores.

The voice of the newscaster on the television almost
lulled her to sleep with her cup of tea resting on her lap.
She was waiting up for a while in order to see the
advertisements during the commercial breaks. It was
part of her job, or at least she'd now made it part of her
job, to keep up to date with the latest ads, to see what
sort of stuff the competition were turning out.

Things would level off, she supposed, as far as work
was concerned. Things couldn't possibly stay as hectic
as they'd been over the past couple of weeks. There
were several jobs she'd had to do during the past
fortnight which wouldn't be in the normal run of things
. . . like arranging the party, for instance.

There had been a meeting of the new Board. Zac and
his Directors, who were hand-picked and the cream of
the London advertising scene, had decided that a party
would be given at Bryant's during the last week of July,
no expense spared. All the clients, big and small, were
to be invited, together with a number of potential
clients, certain members of the press, various contacts
of Zac's and anyone else whose name ought to be
included. The guest list amounted to more than a
hundred names and it was Cindy's task to organise the
entire affair. Of course, everyone who mattered already
knew that Bryant's had been taken over by Zac Stone.
The party was by way of an official announcement.

Cindy didn't wake up of her own accord. At a
little after eight on the Saturday morning she was
wrenched from her sleep by a great, rumbling boom of
thunder immediately overhead. Perspiration broke out
on her forehead. She'd always been terrified of storms.
She stuck her head under her pillow as white flashes of

lightning illuminated her bedroom, making everything appear iridescent.

It was illogical to be afraid, she was aware of that; this was just the price to be paid for the unusually long spell of hot weather lately. But logic didn't help in this instance. The storm raged for over an hour, and as much as she was longing for a cup of coffee, Cindy stayed right where she was.

By lunchtime the storm had long since passed, but it was still pouring with rain. Any hopes of her spending a leisurely day out of doors were shot. But at least the storm had cooled things down a little. After chatting for an hour with her mother on the phone, she slipped into denims and a tee-shirt, and caught up with the housework. She was ironing when the porter buzzed her in the middle of the afternoon.

She picked up the internal telephone in the hall, hoping she wasn't about to have unexpected company. 'Yes, Bill?'

There was a smile in the porter's voice. 'There's a delivery boy from the florist's here, Miss Hetherington. May I send him up?'

Flowers? It wasn't her birthday. 'Er—yes, please do.'

The flowers were from James and they were roses. Twelve of them. Twelve glorious red roses. Cindy had to say one thing for him: he didn't give up easily. Earlier in the week, he'd tried to contact her at the office, but Alison had taken the call. Now he was sending flowers. Her first thought was to drop the entire bouquet down the rubbish chute, but there was no way she could bring herself actually to do it. Her love of all things natural wouldn't allow her to do that. Besides, the roses were innocent, and very beautiful. She placed them carefully into a vase of water and found just the right spot for them in the lounge.

'Forgive me,' the card said, 'James'. Cindy tore it to shreds and went back to the ironing board.

By Sunday afternoon there was no let-up in the weather. It was still raining cats and dogs, but Cindy took herself off to the cinema regardless. She liked her own company well enough, but spending two consecutive days alone indoors was not her idea of a nice weekend. On the way home from the cinema she picked up half a dozen magazines and spent a couple of hours after dinner reading all the ads.

She was getting into bed when the doorbell rang and not only was she naked, she was puzzled. It was almost eleven o'clock and she certainly wasn't expecting company at this hour. It had to be one of her neighbours, unlikely though that was. In all the time Cindy had lived in Priory Court, nobody had said more than good morning or good evening to her. City life was like that.

The security in the building was good. The tenants' privacy was protected. No one got into the building unless they'd been seen and cleared by the porter in the reception area. But when Cindy peered through the tiny spy-hole in her front door, she realised that the security system was by no means infallible. It wasn't one of her neighbours. It was Zac Stone.

'Zac?' she called to him through the closed door. 'Give me a moment, will you? I'm—I'm . . . I was just in the bathroom.' Dashing quickly to her bedroom, she pulled on the nearest garment she could lay her hands on. It was a full-length housecoat in pale blue and perfectly respectable, if not quite the sort of garment she'd choose to wear in her boss's company.

Cindy tied a firm knot in the belt at the waist before opening the door. 'Zac . . . Well, I must say you were the last person I was expecting—not that I was expecting anyone!' She forced a smile, chattering on a little nervously. It was strange, seeing him like this, seeing him out of context, sort of thing. She'd only ever seen him wearing a suit until now.

He looked almost menacing tonight. In a black shirt and black slacks, the depth of his tan was accentuated. His hair was as black as night; it was neither straight nor curly, there was just plenty of it and it was brushed back carelessly from his face. Yes, he did look menacing. Dark and menacing. He also looked very attractive; Cindy admitted it to herself almost reluctantly.

Zac Stone had the sort of face which became more interesting the more one got to know it. The cleft in the chin was very slight, the line of his jaw clearly defined. It was a lean face, a strong face, and the depth of colour in his eyes was quite unlike anything Cindy had seen before. They were so positively blue—deep blue. She could spend a long time looking at that face, enjoying it—if it belonged to someone other than Zac Stone.

'How—how did you get past the doorman?'

Zac walked ahead of her into the living room, not waiting to be invited. 'I nodded and bade him good evening. You don't mind if I sit down, do you?'

'Of course not.' What else could she say? For an instant she wondered how he'd known her exact address, then she remembered his amazing memory and the personnel file. 'What—what can I do for you?' She switched on a couple of lamps as he sat down.

'Two things. No, three.' His eyes moved round the room as he spoke, taking in all its details from the beige carpet to the plants hanging from the ceiling, the cane coffee tables and the sandy-coloured three-piece suite. They lingered momentarily on the roses. His scrutiny was swift, but Cindy knew he'd have missed nothing. 'Were you in bed just now?'

'On my way.' She was unsure whether to remain standing or whether to sit. What did he want with her at this time of night? 'Would you . . . perhaps you'd like a cup of coffee?'

'I'd like a jar of coffee, if you've got one to spare.'

'I'm sorry?' She looked at him blankly.

'It's the traditional thing, isn't it?' He smiled then, looking her over from head to foot as he did so. 'New neighbours usually knock and beg a cup of sugar or a packet of tea from the person next door, don't they?'

'New—*You've* moved in next door?'

'About five minutes ago. I've been living in a hotel while the place was being made ready for me. My furniture was delivered yesterday, but I've been out of town for the weekend. I've just got back now.'

He was enjoying the shock on her face, she could see it in his eyes. She'd seen the furniture van the day before, she'd even felt sorry for the men whose task it had been to unload it in the rain. But she hadn't dreamt that her new neighbour would turn out to be her boss!

'You needn't look unhappy about it, Cindy. From my point of view it could be very convenient having my secretary living next door.'

And very inconvenient from Cindy's point of view. Didn't she put in enough hours of work as it was? 'I'm not unhappy about it.' She lied because she felt it was necessary. Well, it was a half-lie. She didn't exactly feel unhappy about him living next door, she just wasn't thrilled by the idea.

The spark of laughter faded from his eyes. 'Liar,' he challenged, 'why don't you say what's going through your mind?'

'I was just . . . I was just wondering why you never mentioned you were moving into Priory Court.'

'What? And spoil the surprise?' He did it again, just as he had a moment ago. He looked her over from head to foot, but this time he did it slowly, insolently.

It was guaranteed to put Cindy's back up because she knew he was doing it deliberately. She was well aware that on a personal level her boss disapproved of her. Why else would he do it to her? It wasn't as if he were looking at her because she was a woman, it was as if he were thinking—well, she didn't want to speculate on that.

Lifting her head proudly, she took his scrutiny with dignity. She wouldn't give him the satisfaction of a reaction. She took it because she wanted to get on with her job, which was the only reason she made such an effort to get on with Zac Stone.

'You offered me a cup of coffee a moment ago,' he said quietly, sardonically. 'Or do you intend to pose like that all evening, with the lamplight shining through your gown?'

Dumbstruck, Cindy marched from the room and headed for the kitchen. She was blushing to the roots of her hair. She had been standing in front of the light, but she hadn't thought about it for one minute! She glared angrily in the direction of the living room as the sound of Zac's low, rumbling laughter reached her. The nerve of the man! He'd accused her of *posing*! God, he was smart, putting the onus on her when it was his fault she'd stood defiantly rooted to the spot.

She couldn't even remember what she'd come into the kitchen for, she was too busy looking down at her housecoat. It wasn't all that thin; it probably wasn't transparent at all. Was it? But if she slipped into her bedroom and put her underclothes on, it would only amuse Zac Stone all the more. Damn him!

'On second thoughts,' he called, the amusement still there in his voice, 'make it a Scotch, will you? Neat. With ice.'

Fuming, Cindy looked in cupboards for the bottle of whisky she knew she had somewhere. She never touched the stuff herself. With an effort she composed herself before she took him his drink. 'I haven't got a spare jar of coffee. I opened a new one yesterday. I've put some in a small tin for you.'

'Fine.'

She handed him the Scotch. During the past two weeks she'd come to the conclusion that 'thank you' was not in his vocabulary. At least, not when he was speaking to her.

'Aren't you joining me, Cindy?' he asked.

'I don't drink.'

'You do drink.'

'I only drink wine.' It was all she could do to look at him, she was so angry. She sat well away from him, arranging her housecoat so that not even her ankles were showing. 'What else did you want, Zac? You said there were three things.'

His eyebrows rose slightly, but he said nothing more for several seconds. Then he nodded towards the roses. 'Secret admirer?'

'Why secret?' she said stiffly.

'There's no card, your birthday's not till the twelfth of September and you told me quite categorically that you haven't got a boy-friend. At the interview, remember?'

'I remember.' Did she ever!

'Well?'

'I bought them myself.' She was damned if she'd tell him where the roses came from.

'How interesting,' he said drily. 'You went out yesterday in the pouring rain to buy yourself a dozen red roses.'

Cindy looked down at the carpet. It was very obvious the roses were no more than a day old. She put on her bored look and hoped for the best. She wished he would go. The strain between them was almost tangible tonight.

He was just looking at her, and though his face was impassive Cindy could feel his annoyance. 'I was wondering who does your cleaning for you. That was the second thing I wanted. If your cleaning lady isn't occupied elsewhere perhaps you'd ask her to come and do my place when she's finished in here. I want someone to come in every day. Weekdays, that is.'

'I do my own housework. But if you ask the porter, he'll make the necessary arrangements for you.'

'I'm surprised you know how.' Zac smiled slightly, but it didn't lessen the sarcasm in his voice. He looked around the room. 'But you evidently do.'

His remark stung, but Cindy was determined not to give him any feedback. Did he think she'd been wrapped up in cotton wool all her life? 'And the third thing you wanted?'

The muscles of his face tightened almost imperceptibly. 'You know, we've spent many hours together, but we've never had a conversation.'

'There's no time for conversation at work.'

He corrected her. 'What you mean is that you have no time for conversation. There's a difference.'

'I . . . didn't say that.'

'Well? We're not at work now. So why don't you say what's really going through your mind?'

Cindy was growing more anxious, and angry, by the minute. She was suspicious of him, of what he wanted. Had he come here hoping to catch her off guard? Was he spoiling for a fight? She wouldn't be surprised. 'It—I don't think that would be a good idea. Why don't we just leave things as they are? You're my boss, Zac. We get the job done. That's all we need to be concerned about really.'

'But we're neighbours, too. Remember? And I want to know more about my new neighbour . . .'

He was goading her again. And the more he did it, the more angry she became. He was lounging on her sofa, his legs stretched out before him and his arms spread out across the backrest. His presence seemed to fill the room, but it had little to do with the sheer size of him. Cindy felt threatened, dominated, even claustrophobic.

'. . . Let's take this room, for instance. This is an unusual sort of room, Cindy. It tells me quite a lot about you.'

Cindy's control was starting to slip. 'Does it? I should have thought you knew enough about me already.'

'Oh, no.' He said it quietly, too quietly. 'Not yet.' He smiled, the darkness of his skin making his teeth seem even whiter. But the smile didn't touch his eyes. 'I can't really say I like the room. Obviously it's too feminine for my liking, but it's pretty much as I expected it to be. It shows taste, it's expensively furnished and it's . . . cool.'

If there was a compliment somewhere in his last sentence, his tone had turned it into a backhanded one. Cindy got to her feet quickly. 'I'll get your coffee.'

She walked out briskly. What did he know about taste? After the way he'd had their offices decorated, she dreaded to think what he'd had done to the flat next door. She snatched up the coffee—only to walk smack into him as she was leaving the kitchen. Obviously his curiosity was such that he wanted to see what the rest of her flat looked like.

Zac's arms came out to steady her on her feet and Cindy took an involuntary step backwards. His touch came as a shock to her, and it was more than she could manage to hide the fact. The small tin of coffee dropped from her fingers and scattered over the kitchen floor. Neither of them noticed it. Alarmed at her reaction to the physical contact, at the way her pulses leapt in response, she felt her shoulders tense as her eyes met with his. Zac's eyes looked deeply into hers, moving downwards over her face as though he'd never seen it before. His strong fingers were burning against the flesh of her arms through the soft material of her housecoat. It seemed as if minutes passed before he let go of her but in reality it was only seconds. Seconds. Just a few seconds in which he was holding her so close that she could feel the warmth of his breath on her cheek.

But they were seconds that Cindy regretted.

Zac Stone was undeniably attractive. There was an innate strength, an animal magnetism about the man that had struck her from the moment she'd set eyes on him. He was very much the physical type, a man whom no woman would pass by without turning to take a second look.

But there was nothing else attractive about him. He was ruthless through and through. He was hard, insensitive and the very epitome of everything Cindy disliked in a man. She stepped away from him smartly, her hands going up to her arms where his fingers had touched her flesh. She regretted he'd had reason to touch her. She regretted the physical effect it had had on her. But she didn't realise how much that regret showed on her face, didn't realise how her soft mouth had grown taut, how her head had tilted upwards as if she would defy her own response.

'You bitch!' Suddenly, all hell broke loose as the deep voice hissed at her. 'You haughty, supercilious little bitch!' he grabbed hold of her so roughly that she cried out in pain. In one swift, continuous movement his lips came down on her open mouth as his fingers bit hard into her arms.

Cindy's lips parted further as pain shot through her, but her cry was smothered, drowned by the punishment of his kiss. It was more than she could endure, but she was not afraid of him. She absolutely was not afraid of him! It took everything she had to wrench her body sideways in an effort to break the contact of his lips. 'You bastard! How dare you——'

'How *dare* I?' Zac's eyes glinted dangerously. 'So you're too snooty to be touched, are you? Too haughty to be kissed! You've pushed me too far tonight, with your bored expression and your filthy looks!'

'What the hell are you talking about? You listen— oh!' Cindy gasped in frustration at the ease with which he yanked her closer towards him. She was crushed against the hardness of his chest as he claimed her mouth once more, her arms and her back immobilised by his vice-like grip. The force of his mouth on hers made her lips part involuntarily. He kissed her mercilessly, bruisingly, until her mind was screaming in indignation, humiliation. But somewhere deep inside her there was a response, in spite of everything. In spite of the way he was hurting her, in spite of the hatred she was feeling for him.

'I'm going to change this attitude of yours, madam, if it's the last thing I do.' When at last he raised his head Cindy was gasping for breath and still struggling frantically to free herself. 'Stop struggling, damn you! You'll get more of what you've just had unless you keep still and listen to me!'

The volume of his voice made her flinch then, but she glared at him defiantly, her brown eyes wide and darkened with anger. 'What's the matter with you? You're crazy! Let me *go*!' She twisted violently, freeing her right arm. Her hand flew upwards towards Zac's face, but it was caught by the wrist in mid-air. Her efforts were wasted. She'd known that all along, but her pride and her fury would not allow her to succumb.

Zac swore and lifted her bodily, moving her further back until she was pinned against the sink. His eyes were sparking with rage as he pushed both her arms behind her, holding them in the small of her back with one hand. 'If you try anything like that again, you'll find yourself on the receiving end. Now keep still and listen to me!'

She had no choice. His feet were set apart as he towered over her, his body only inches from her own. The steel of the sink was pressing against her lower back as he held her in place with the grip on her wrists. 'All right, all right! But let go of me, *please*!'

'I thought I told you to shut up . . .' He bent his head and Cindy drew her breath in sharply as she saw what was coming.

'No! Please! All right. Zac, for God's sake!'

He straightened, looking down at her with anger which was barely contained. 'This has been brewing for the past two weeks, Cindy. You know that as well as I do. I intend to clear the air once and for all. I'm sick of the atmosphere between us, I'm sick of your patronising little smiles, your disdainful looks, your entire *attitude*.'

'*My* attitude? You've got a nerve! You can't speak to me without drenching your words with sarcasm——'

'Not sarcasm. Bluntness. I believe in calling a spade a spade.'

'That isn't true!' she countered. 'If that were true, if you were honest, you'd say it directly. You'd tell me to my face that you resent my independence, you resent my background!'

She saw his brows pull together in a frown. 'Don't

talk such rubbish!' he said angrily. 'What the hell has that got to do with anything?'

'You didn't want to give me the job in the first place . . . Zac, my back's hurting! Please let me go. If you really want to talk . . . I can't think straight like this. Let's—let's sit down.'

'You'll stay right where you are. This suits me just fine.' He released her at once, but he made sure she didn't move by stepping a little closer to her. Just inches. But they were inches that closed the space between their bodies so that the tips of her breasts were brushing against him. And then he kissed her again before she could even guess his intention. Cindy's mind spun in confusion. She couldn't begin to understand him, his behaviour . . . But his kiss was quite different now. It didn't last and it didn't punish.

'What . . . what was that for? I—I didn't——' She was tongue-tied, confused and very, very disturbed by the feelings he aroused in her, by the warmth which suffused her body, by the utterly ridiculous urge she had to reach out and pull him towards her so that his mouth would once again claim hers. This, while at the same time her intellect was telling her to strike out at him for all she was worth. But she didn't move a muscle.

Zac was smiling, but there was no humour in it. 'That was for being a good girl. For telling me, finally, what's been bugging you, what's been going through your mind. I've invited you to do that umpteen times before tonight, Cindy, but all I've had is a stony silence, that hauteur, that special brand of disdain you're so practised at giving.'

The smile faded, to be replaced by straightforward irritation. But at least, thank heavens, it wasn't anger. 'Now let's make this quite clear: It's all I've just described which irritates the hell out of me. As for your accusation—your history, your independence or whatever you called it doesn't enter into things as far as I'm concerned. I'm neither resentful of it nor impressed by it. But you yourself allow those things to spoil you. You're snooty, stuck-up, cold and unnatural. I like straight talk, Cindy. There's a dishonesty in your attitude—in your *withholding*—that I'm not prepared to tolerate. Do you understand?'

She did and she didn't. It had come as a shock to her to hear herself described by Zac as he saw her. Yet she began to understand, now, how she'd managed to give him that impression ... such a *wrong* impression. If only he knew her, really! She'd been working on a false assumption about his resentment. He *had* resented her, but not for the reasons ... oh, if only she had more time to think, to sort it all out in her mind. But it was too late, by the look of it. Disappointment overtook her then, and it showed. 'So—so you're telling me I've just talked myself out of a job. You've finally found——'

Zac sighed, long and hard. 'Are we having a semantic problem now or are you being deliberately obtuse?'

'Zac, I don't understand—you said ... Oh, I don't understand *you*!'

'Evidently. Which is precisely the problem between us. I'm not firing you, for heaven's sake! Am I likely to fire you for speaking your mind, for doing exactly what I want you to do? Besides, I never let go of people who are potentially useful to me. Potentially, mark you. You've a lot to learn about your job yet, but I'm satisfied with your progress so far. You were on trial for one month, and that's how it stays. But from now on you'll loosen up a little. You're part of a team, my team, and I don't like strained atmospheres in the office.'

Cindy looked up at him in silence. Zac Stone was really a ...

'Say it!' Zac turned his hands palms upwards, shrugging. 'Just say it.'

'I—I was thinking you—you really are an extraordinary man. But my God, I dislike you!'

The blue eyes warmed with laughter and his smile parted his lips. 'Now there's a very good girl!'

Without warning, he took her in his arms and kissed her passionately. He kissed her with a passion she had known all along he was capable of. And it frightened the life out of her. Instinctively she'd inched away from him, the free part of her body swaying backwards, but Zac's arms came round her back and pulled her easily but firmly against his chest.

This time, Cindy's lips were parted by the insistence of the kiss. He kissed her slowly but hungrily, probing, exploring until her senses reeled and everything that had happened, everything that had previously passed between them faded into nothingness. She was aware only of this moment, of the hard pressure of his body against hers. In response to her unspoken longing, his hands came round to cup her breasts, his fingers moving in a slow, exquisitely sensuous rhythm.

There was no resistance in her. Cindy couldn't have stopped him if she'd wanted to. She was frightened by that knowledge and she was ashamed at her own reaction, at the way she had responded so readily, even hungrily. All too soon, it was over, and Zac stepped away from her, smiling at the way her cheeks suffused with colour as he looked into her eyes. It was a smile of satisfaction.

Cindy simply didn't know what to do, what to say. She couldn't know how she looked, with her lips moist and parted, her dark eyes telling him far, far more than she wanted him to know. Unlike Zac, she wasn't smiling. Unlike him, she was bewildered. Never, *never* had she reacted physically to a man the way she had reacted to him.

She'd felt Zac's response as plainly as she'd felt her own. She watched, now, as his breathing slowed back to normal. But he was fully in control. Oh, so coolly, completely in control. Just as he had been all along, since setting foot inside her flat, since the moment they'd met.

He'd won. And she hated him for it. She was glad the air had been cleared, she was glad she was now free to be herself . . . But Zac Stone had a different hold over her now. A different power. A power she wasn't able to resist.

And he knew it.

She tore her eyes from his. 'I . . . Zac . . . the coffee. I'll get you some more.'

'Forget it. I can live through one breakfast without coffee. Goodnight, Cindy. I'll see you tomorrow.' He turned, but she called his name.

'I—was this what you came for tonight? To clear the air, I mean. Was it all premeditated?'

'Actually, no.' He shrugged slightly, and she believed him. 'You asked for it tonight. But it was on the agenda, I can't deny that.'

'But the third thing. Was it . . . this?' She pulled her gown more closely around her, looking away.

Zac's laugh was short. 'No, it wasn't that. That wasn't premeditated, either. I wanted to mention that I've got a list of nine more names to add to those of the people we've invited to the party. Remind me to give it to you tomorrow.'

She nodded, still avoiding his eyes. 'All right.'

'Now there's a good girl!'

Like one conditioned, Cindy responded to those words with alarm written all over her lovely face.

'Relax!' Zac threw back his head and laughed. 'We'll deal with one thing at a time, Cindy. One thing at a time.'

With that, he left, and Cindy stood rooted to the spot, staring after him. He'd surprised her over and over again tonight, and she still had a lot to sort out in her mind. But Zac Stone's last remark was a cryptic one. Quite what he'd meant by it she couldn't be sure.

But she certainly had her suspicions.

CHAPTER FOUR

As Cindy walked to work on the morning of the day of the party she reflected on the way her life—at least her working life—had changed dramatically in such a short space of time. It was the last Friday of July—and the last day of her one-month trial period.

The new Bryant's was so different from the old. She was surrounded by interesting people, in an interesting job. Working for someone other than Zac couldn't possibly have been the same. In her job she had found what she'd been looking for.

Things were going well. Life was so much easier now she was able to be herself with Zac. As far as everyone else was concerned she and Zac were part of a team, all of whom had a basic respect for one another. When in the presence of other members of staff, Cindy treated Zac in precisely that manner.

But from time to time, in their private moments, the old animosity would raise its head. Or perhaps it was simply a clash of personalities. Whatever, at least she was free to speak her mind now, when that happened. So there was no strain between them. The only strain that Cindy was currently experiencing was that which was a natural byproduct of working hard and long hours. But she didn't mind that, and if her social life was non-existent, she didn't even notice.

And yet, while one difficulty with Zac had been resolved, another one had taken its place. But that was only as far as Cindy was concerned, and it was a far more controllable problem. She was acutely aware of Zac as a man. And she didn't want to be. She wanted only to think of him as her boss, and prior to the showdown with him it had been easy to do that. Now, however, it was difficult indeed to think of him only in those terms.

As a slow drizzle started to fall, Cindy edged closer to the wall as she walked. So much for the weather forecast! She didn't even have her umbrella with her. It wasn't that she disliked getting wet, it was that she hated the way her hair went very curly in the rain—and there'd be no chance whatever of having it blow-dried before the party. Today was going to be hectic, to say the least.

Quite apart from checking that everything was in order for the party that evening, she had a pile of day-to-day work waiting for her. Bryant's was buzzing at the moment because a new campaign was being planned—thanks to the new boss.

Come to think of it, she did respect Zac Stone—in a purely professional sense, that is. Zac doubled as the Creative Director. He did that because he was an advertising man down to his fingertips, and working mainly as an administrator would not have given him the pleasure he so obviously derived from being in on the action. The instigator of the action.

He had done a superb job on the Simpson account. Simpson's were manufacturers of furniture and they had warehouses in every major city from which they sold direct to the public. They advertised through television, radio and the press, and they spent vast sums of money. It was big business, Bryant's biggest account. And Bryant's had been in danger of losing them.

Simpson's factory and head office were in Middlesex, and it had been there that the meeting had taken place during which Zac Stone had not only prevented the loss of this account but sold them on the idea of an entirely new advertising campaign on a nationwide scale. Greg Halliday and Cindy had watched him do it.

Greg Halliday was one of the new men Zac had brought in. He had been appointed Senior Account Director and had done a great deal of talking at the meeting with Simpson's, whose account he would be in charge of. But it was Zac's reputation as the best TV advertising man in the business that had pulled it off.

Whereas old Mr Bryant had been very much a newspaper man, behind the times as far as TV advertising was concerned, it was in the latter that Zac Stone's real expertise lay. Greg had told Cindy this, and coming from him it was undoubtedly high praise. Greg was cast very much in the same mould as Zac; he knew the ad business inside out, though physically and personality-wise the two men could not have been more different.

Cindy's reappraisal of the past four weeks was interrupted when Zac's car slowed down beside her. He opened the passenger door and called to her, 'Hop in.'

But the damage was already done as far as Cindy's hair was concerned. She moved towards the car, but declined the offer of a lift. Zac had offered her a lift only once before, and she had explained to him that she preferred to walk to the office. On two evenings after work she had actually asked for a lift, simply because she had been too tired to walk. And after all, he did live next door to her.

Apart from those two instances, though, Zac might just as well have lived on the other side of London. As a neighbour she never saw him. He seemed to disappear during the weekends and he had never impinged on her private time except for the evening when he had asked for the coffee.

'No, thanks. I don't mind getting wet. You know I like my morning constitutional—it's the only peaceful time of the day.' Not for the first time, Cindy was thinking how very fitting it was that her boss drove a black Jaguar. She could think of no other car that would suit him better than a Jaguar. It was black, it was sleek and sophisticated . . . and it could be lethal if badly handled.

'I don't mind if you get wet, either,' he came back at her. 'You can get soaked to the skin for all I care. I'm concerned about you getting to work on time. You're

running late and we've got a hell of a lot to do today—
so get in this car, and fast! I don't want to pick up a
reputation as a pavement crawler.'

She got in.

'Food, Cindy. You never told me what you'd
arranged with the caterers for the party. Of course, it's
a bit late to make changes now.' Zac pulled away
smoothly and swiftly. How he coped with the morning
rush hour in the West End, Cindy couldn't imagine. It
was more than she'd like to tackle every day. Still, at
least he had a parking spot in town.

'Now why should I bother a busy man like yourself
with a detail such as that? The invitations were sent out
by me, the drinks, the bar, the food, everything was left
up to me, remember? You said spare no expense, and
get on with it. So I did.'

'Point taken, point taken,' he laughed. 'And no doubt
your taste in food is as impeccable as your taste in
clothes.'

Cindy looked at him sideways. That sounded very
much like a compliment.

'Don't you ever give that car of yours a run? That is
your car, isn't it, the white Spitfire that never moves off
the forecourt?'

'Yes. I'm afraid it's been neglected of late.' Cindy was
attempting to smooth down her hair. She could feel the
feathery little curls framing her face already. If only
she'd picked up her umbrella . . .

'But you told me at the interview you sometimes
"pop down to the coast and spend the weekend by the
sea".'

She looked at him sideways again. Not only had he
quoted her verbatim, he had also used the same
inflection she had used. 'So I did. And I did pop down
to the coast quite often. But frankly it's taken me some
time to adjust to my new pace of work. I've been
sleeping during the weekends—recharging my batteries,
so to speak. Mind you, I really must make an effort. I
do like to get out of London at weekends.'

'Same here,' he nodded. 'I'm house-hunting at the moment. I'm looking for a place in the country—somewhere I can make an escape to at the weekends.'

'You surprise me, actually. You seem so much a City man. I didn't think you'd have the urge to get away from it.'

Zac shrugged, manoeuvring the big car into the small, tightly-packed parking lot with enviable ease. 'I never used to have that urge. One changes, Cindy. Besides, I think when one's country-born, at some point in one's life the attractions of the countryside always come back and beckon.'

She was about to say that she hadn't realised he was country-born. She knew he was Welsh, of course, but that was the sum total of Cindy's knowledge of Zac Stone—outside the advertising world.

But Zac was already getting out of the car. He came round and opened the passenger door for her—and immediately succeeded in spoiling her good mood by telling her the rain had made her hair curl. 'I'm well aware of it,' she said shortly. 'And you're about to tell me I look like Goldilocks, right?'

Zac made an expansive gesture with his arms. 'Now would I say something like that when it would obviously upset you?'

'Yes.'

'Besides, it's Sheila who's labelled you Goldilocks . . . Well, that's one of your nicknames, anyway.'

'I know, I know.' They were walking quickly towards the office in an effort to escape the rain, which was now getting heavier by the minute. Cindy was well aware of her other nickname—Miss Cool. She smiled inwardly, wondering if Zac was aware of the name he'd been allocated by Sheila. Zac Stone was not Sheila's favourite person.

Zac's strides were impossible to keep up with. He was several yards ahead of Cindy when next he spoke.

'I didn't hear a word of that,' she said breathlessly. ''Would you mind slowing down if you want to make small talk?'

He turned and grinned, waiting for her to catch up with him. 'I said I'll bet you're glad I gave you a lift now, considering the weather. Come to think of it, if I gave you a lift every morning, you'd have more energy for the job. It's silly to waste your energy on walking.'

'Thanks.'

Zac's blue eyes were laughing as he and Cindy entered the foyer of the building. He punched the lift button. 'If it comes to that, it's even sillier that we're both paying an extortionate rent when two can live as cheaply as one. Why don't you move in next door?'

'Thanks, but no thanks. I'd rather live with a rattlesnake.'

At which Zac Stone threw back his head and roared with laughter. 'Why, Cynthia, how very Freudian!'

She glared at him all the way up to the second floor.

By four in the afternoon Cindy had a pounding headache. The guests were due to arrive any time after five-thirty. She had yet to go home and change, and she was in the Boardroom, checking on the caterers' movements, when Zac came looking for her.

'Cindy, where the hell have you put that stuff you fished out of the library for me?'

'The old Eleanor ads?'

'Of course the old Eleanor ads! What else did you fish out of the library today?'

Cindy looked up from the list of foodstuffs she was checking off. 'They're on your desk, Zac.'

He grunted. 'How many times have I told you not to tidy up my office?'

'Twice.'

'And you persist——'

'Only when I walk in there and trip over things.'

Zac walked away without another word and Cindy turned back to her list. He had this weird system of running his office. There were charts and files and a hundred other such items of reference strewn all over the place—mainly on the floor. But he knew exactly where everything was . . . unless some well-meaning idiot moved something. Cindy shrugged it off. There was too much to do without thinking about things like that.

When she told Zac she wanted to go home and change, he went up in the air. 'You must be joking! Forget it. There's no time for that. Besides, you know it isn't that sort of party. No one's going to be dressed up—they're all coming from their offices.'

Cindy put her foot down. 'Zac, I insist. I'll be very quick, I promise. I feel so—so crumpled. I must at least pick up a fresh blouse. I'll take a taxi——'

Zac looked heavenwards, fished in his pocket and threw his car keys at her. 'Take my car—and be quick about it. You've got twenty minutes to get there and back. I want you here when people start to arrive.'

It took Cindy forty-five minutes to get there and back. It would have been quicker to walk than to plough her way nervously through the traffic in an unfamiliar car. A car which didn't belong to her, at that. She bolted up to her second floor flat and grabbed a black blouse which was sleeveless and very sheer. She'd worn a white blouse and a black pencil skirt to the office that day—so the skirt would do.

With the blouse on a hanger she raced downstairs again and got back to the office in what she considered record time.

'It took you long enough.' Zac emerged from his office as Cindy hung up her blouse on the stationery cupboard.

She cast him an apologetic look and turned to Alison, who was just preparing to leave. 'Alison, would you do me a favour before you go? Would you get me a couple of Paracetamol from the first aid box? I've got a dreadful headache.'

'Of course! I'm sorry you've got a headache, Cindy.' Alison's shyness had been diminishing by the day. She was no longer tongue-tied and flustered in Zac's presence, though she still looked at him as if he were wonderful.

Zac took the car keys Cindy was holding out to him. 'Alison, aren't you staying to the party?'

'No, Mr Stone. Very few of the junior staff are. I mean, it is Friday night——'

'And they have better things to do, I suppose. Quite right.' Zac smiled at her.

'Actually, I've got a date tonight.' For Alison, this was really quite something, and Cindy looked up in surprise, smiling.

'I'm not surprised,' Zac said smoothly. 'You look very nice today, Alison. That's a new dress, isn't it? And you've lost some more weight this week.'

Alison beamed at him. 'Another four pounds. It's slow but it's sure.'

'And it's paying dividends, eh? Anyone I know, this date of yours?'

'Oh, I don't think so, Mr Stone. It isn't someone who works here.'

'All right,' Zac shrugged. 'Be mysterious, then.'

Alison laughed and went off to fetch the Paracetamol.

'Oh, no! Cindy turned to Zac, a look of horror on her face. 'Zac, give me back the keys. I've forgotten something!'

'What?'

'I've got to nip home again. Give me your car keys.'

'You've had that!' he said firmly. 'What have you forgotten? It's bound to be something trivial!'

'My——' Cindy tutted impatiently. Bother the man. 'My bra. I forgot to pick up another bra. I can't wear a white one with a black blouse!'

Zac started to walk away from her. 'So go braless.'

'Zac!'

He turned and grinned, looking from her distraught face to the white blouse she had on to the sheer black silk blouse hanging on the cupboard. 'I see what you mean.' He laughed, shrugged, and went into his office.

'No problem,' he called to her. 'Give me a minute.'

Cindy couldn't imagine what he meant. She sank wearily on to her chair and started massaging her temples. She looked up to see Zac standing there dangling two bras on one of his fingers. 'Flesh-coloured or black?' he mused, asking himself more than he was asking Cindy.

She couldn't help laughing. 'Are those the new Eleanor samples? The ones that came for the photographic session?'

'Yes. They sent a whole boxful of goodies . . . all sizes, shapes and colours. Here.' He handed Cindy the black bra and she stood up to take it from him.

Zac immediately caught hold of her by the waist, holding her tightly against him. His face was dangerously close to hers, and Cindy felt her heartbeat quicken. 'Unless appearances deceive . . .' he said slowly, an insolent smile pulling at the corners of his mouth, '. . . or should I say, unless I'm losing my touch, this will fit you perfectly.'

Cindy flushed with embarrassment at the memory he invoked. She wriggled to try and free herself, but it only made Zac's smile broaden. 'Mmm, that's nice. How very provocative of you, Cindy!'

She put both hands flat on his chest and tried to push him away. 'Zac, let go of me! I have to get changed!'

But Zac kept hold of her, his hands sliding down to her hips. 'Is there anything else you've forgotten?' he asked, his deep blue eyes dancing with laughter. 'I've got all sorts of things in my sample box.'

'Zac! Oh, really, you . . . you're . . . absolutely incorrigible!'

He let go of her then. He slipped his forefinger under her chin and tilted her face upwards, looking directly into her eyes. 'Not incorrigible, Cindy, encouragable. Encouragable.'

She opened her mouth to protest, but the office door opened and Alison walked in with the bottle of Paracetamol.

Cindy took them from her, draped her blouse over her arm and stuffed the bra into her handbag. She headed for the ladies' room quickly, still disturbed by the effect Zac's closeness had had on her. Encouragable? Never! Encouraging a man like Zac Stone was the last thing she wanted to do!

The bra fitted perfectly.

By six o'clock the place was thronged with people. It seemed that for every man present there was also a secretary, a wife or a mistress. The continuous chinking of glasses, the tinkle of laughter and the buzz of conversations did nothing whatever to help Cindy's headache.

But she was very much on duty, and no one would have guessed how she was feeling. She was smiling, greeting, chatting, introducing, and generally circulating. She had been briefed by her boss as to whom she should make a fuss of and she'd been told also not to stray too far from him.

She was standing with her back to Zac, among a group of people who included the Chairman of Simpson's, when she heard her boss greet someone very, very warmly.

'Well, well! I'm so glad you could make it. I'm delighted to see you, darling, delighted.' It didn't sound at all like Zac.

Cindy automatically tuned in on the conversation as she heard the tinkle of a woman's laughter. The ability to keep her mind on two things at the same time was something she'd had to learn while working for Zac. She could manage easily to chat to Mr Simpson and listen to what was happening around her.

'Not half as delighted as I am, Zac. But I'm suspicious. Why the invitation?'

'Tracy! I'm deeply offended.'

Cindy turned slightly so she could get a look at the person Zac was talking to. The woman looked somewhere in the region of thirty; she was wearing a red trouser suit which showed off her figure to perfection. It was expensive and beautifully cut, and it suited her colouring. Her straight hair reached almost to her waist and was almost as dark as Zac's. Furthermore, her face was familiar to Cindy—and it was very beautiful. Her bone structure was classical, her make-up doing it the utmost justice, accentuating very cleverly the green, almond-shaped eyes.

But Cindy couldn't remember where she'd seen that face before.

'There's so much I'd like to ask you,' the woman went on. 'I know why you retired, but I don't know why you came out of retirement. I don't know why you didn't contact me as soon as you came back to England. I don't know why you invited me here tonight . . . you're not thinking of picking up where we left off, are you, Zac?'

Cindy didn't hear the answer to that. Greg Halliday, the Senior Account Director, slipped a hand under her elbow and whisked her away, excusing himself and Cindy from the group she'd been chatting to.

'There's someone I want you to meet,' Greg whispered. 'Potential business, I think. Besides, Zac wouldn't want you chatting to Mr Simpson for too long. He'd see no point in it when we've already got Simpson's business!'

The next time she had a chance to look in Zac's direction she saw he was with a short, bald-headed man who was waving his arms about. The two men were standing by themselves, in a corner of the room, and there was a familiar, set look about Zac's face. he was listening and mentally recording every word the other man said. Cindy recognised the look. As far as business was concerned she'd learned to read her boss very well. She had no choice in the matter; she was supposed to be one step ahead of his requirements every minute of the day. But she didn't always succeed.

The sound of Sheila's voice in Cindy's ear some time later was preceded by a soft chuckle. 'Look at her!' Sheila nodded in the direction of the woman Zac had been talking to earlier. 'She can't take her eyes off Granite Face!'

Cindy followed the direction of Sheila's eyes and saw that the woman called Tracy was indeed watching Zac from her seat on the other side of the room. By now, Zac was ensconced in conversation with several other females and a couple of elderly men.

'You know, her face is so familiar,' Cindy said. 'Is she a model?'

'Yes. Well, she was. It's Tracy Lynn, as she called herself professionally. She's just told me she retired recently. Over the hill, I suppose.' Sheila laughed again. 'I hope I look like that when I'm over the hill!'

'Don't be silly, Sheila. She's beautiful.'

'Not enough for the close-up photographic work she used to do. Take a closer look at her if you can.'

Cindy had placed Tracy now. Her face had appeared in countless photographs in women's magazines, modelling for a popular brand of cosmetics. It had been a well-known face a few years ago, but Cindy had seen nothing of it for quite a time.

She was curious to hear more about the woman, but she didn't dare to encourage Sheila. Zac Stone was all for people picking up useful information however and wherever possible but he was dead against general gossip. And in this instance, Cindy had the feeling there might well be room for gossip. The way Tracy and Zac had looked at one another had been . . . well, friendly was putting it mildly.

But Sheila didn't need encouragement. 'Yes, I think Tracy's about Zac's age, actually. I knew her quite well about twelve years ago, when I worked for my first agency. She did some modelling for us—shoes, clothes, that sort of thing. Then she did all that cosmetics work for Zac's old agency. In fact, he really made her career. They're just old friends, I suppose . . . in case you were wondering.'

'I wasn't.' Cindy was lying in her teeth, and Sheila knew it.

'She's well preserved,' Sheila went on. 'You wouldn't think she was a day over thirty, would you?'

But Sheila wasn't being bitchy. She astonished Cindy by adding, 'And she's a really nice person. There's no edge to her, if you know what I mean. Her success and her looks never went to her head. She's really nice.'

Coming from Sheila that was high praise indeed. It wasn't often she didn't pinpoint a fault in a person.

By eighty-thirty Cindy's headache had taken a really firm hold, in spite of a second dose of tablets. She escaped into the privacy of her own office and sat down with her head held slightly forward and her eyes closed. If she could just have ten minutes' relative quiet she might calm herself out of this and feel fit to face more of the hubbub.

'What are you doing, Cindy? Why are you holding your hands like that? Are you trying to invoke more rain or something?'

Cindy opened her eyes slowly at the sound of Zac's voice. He'd obviously seen her make her escape, but he wasn't cross with her. He was laughing.

'It's a yoga exercise.'

'Of course it it,' he said drily. 'I shouldn't ask stupid questions. Come on, let's get out of here.'

She thought he meant they should rejoin the party, but Zac shook his head rather tiredly. 'No. Let's go and have a quiet drink somewhere, eh? I've had quite enough for one day.'

'It sounds good.' Cindy didn't need asking twice. She picked up her bag and they left.

When they were seated in Zac's car, she looked at him closely. 'You're looking very pleased with yourself, Zac. The party seemed to go down well, didn't it?'

'It was money well spent,' he said quietly. 'Very useful indeed.'

His choice of words made Cindy look at him curiously. 'You've learned something of interest, haven't you? It was something that little man said to you.'

Zac took his eyes from the road. 'Now how did you know that?'

'I don't know. I just did.'

'So you've been watching me all evening, have you? Couldn't take your eyes off me, mm?'

'You conceited devil! You told me to keep an eye on you—and not to stray too far.' Cindy laughed in spite of herself.

'How's the head?' he asked.

'Chronic.'

'Did you eat at the party?'

'Not a thing.'

'Did you have lunch?'

She gave him a filthy look. 'You know I didn't. You said there was no time for lunch!'

Zac groaned as if he were appalled. 'What a dreadful employer you've got! I'll buy you dinner, right now. No wonder you've got a headache.'

'No, but thanks anyway.' Cindy touched his arm as he indicated to make a left hand turn which would take them away from home. 'Really, Zac, it's nice of you, but I couldn't face it. I want to be somewhere quiet.'

'Then we'll go somewhere quiet. My place.' He turned left regardless. 'And we'll pick up something on the way.'

'Chinese takeaway? I know a good place——'

'So do I. The same one, no doubt.'

Cindy smiled. Zac was in a particularly good mood tonight and she couldn't help wondering about it. 'Who was he?' she asked.

'Now what are you talking about?'

'You know full well. That little man at the party.'

'Someone who wasn't on the guest list. Someone who had invited himself . . . thank heavens. He's the head of a perfume manufacturing company and he was very disgruntled because his current advertising agency has told him they no longer want his business. They're pitching for business with another, much bigger manufacturer of perfumes and toiletries. The little man is small fry, so they've dropped him.'

This wasn't unusual. Cindy was well aware that the rules of advertising were such that one agency may not handle two accounts which are in direct competition with one another. Nor may they pitch for other business in the same line unless they drop their current customer. If they end up failing to get the new business after all . . . well, that's a chance which agencies had to take. 'So he wants you to handle his advertising in future?'

'Yes, he does.' Zac nodded slowly, his eyes narrowing. 'And I turned him down flat.'

Cindy's lips parted in astonishment. The downhill path Bryant's had been taking prior to Zac Stone stepping in had been arrested when Zac salvaged the Simpson account. Indeed, some new business had come to Zac without him even trying for it. But they were by no means in the position yet of being able to refuse new clients!

'Why on earth did you do that?'

In a tone of voice which Cindy had never heard him use before he said, 'Now then, my lovely, why don't we just forget about business for the rest of this evening?'

Cindy turned to look out of the window, feeling suddenly nervous and a little too warm.

CHAPTER FIVE

As Cindy emerged from Zac's kitchen, having put the rapidly-cooling Chinese food on to plates, she found him in the middle of a telephone conversation.

'. . . I see. Me? Yes, yes, I'm fine, thanks.' He motioned Cindy to put the plates on the coffee table. 'And you and the family? . . . Yes, yes, I suppose they are. Time flies, doesn't it? Anyway, when can I be sure of catching your husband at home? All right, I'll ring then . . . And thank you very much.'

He hung up and sat perfectly still, thoughtful.

'Zac?'

It was seconds before he turned to her. 'I'm sorry, Cindy. What did you say?'

Her head was tilted slightly to one side. 'I hadn't said anything . . .' She was wondering where he'd gone to in his thoughts. 'That was something to do with business, that call, wasn't it? I thought you said you were going to forget about business for the rest of the evening.'

He smiled at her warmly, a little apologetically. 'So I did, so I did. But I'm trying to fix up a meeting with someone and it isn't going to be easy. My only chance is to catch him at home. But he's away for a few days.'

Cindy was intrigued—by Zac, and whatever it was he was up to. 'Are you going to tell your secretary about it?' Softly, though she was in little doubt about the answer, she added, 'You do trust me, don't you?'

It was the last Friday of the month, and Cindy had been given her pay cheque that morning. She had been given a substantial raise, but she was more pleased about the implications than the raise in salary. It meant she was no longer on trial.

Zac looked at her steadily, his voice very serious.

'Yes, Cindy. I trust you implicitly.' He got to his feet and shrugged off his jacket, loosening his tie, just as he wore it in the office when there were no clients around. But there was something different about him tonight. Seeing him in his home was probably the reason for that. In fact Zac's flat had in itself been quite a revelation to her.

He went over to the bar and picked up a couple of glasses and a bottle of red wine. 'But I don't want to tempt providence by talking about my plans. As it is, they're likely to go up in smoke at any moment.'

Cindy nodded, understanding what he meant. He'd tell her when he was ready to tell her. She picked up her plate and started eating. 'The food's almost cold.'

'Yes, I'm sorry about that. Here, this'll help it down.'

After she had taken a sip of wine, Cindy's eyes went straight to the label on the bottle. It was expensive, delicious and far too good to accompany what they were eating. She said as much, but Zac just laughed and said hang the expense.

They ate in silence. Cindy was particular about what she ate, but she finished every last bit of it simply because she was ravenous. It was only when she cleared the plates away that she mentioned her surprise at the way the flat was decorated. 'You've had a completely new kitchen put in! So that's what all the banging was about. It's super.'

'I'm afraid it's wasted on me, really.'

'You know, I thought your home would resemble something like the inside of a spaceship.'

Zac had stretched out on the four-seater chesterfield settee. It was covered in brown leather, with two matching chairs. The bar in the corner of the room was made from mahogany, as were the coffee tables. The walls were the colour of eggshells, relieved by several paintings which were classics and rich in colour. The light from the lamps was subdued, as was the colour of the carpet—a rich, dark shade of rust. But it was just right; it added colour to a room which would otherwise have been too dark.

Zac didn't seem to understand her. 'Why did you think that?'

'The way you had our offices decorated—that appalling red on my walls. Of course, I know what's behind that. Red is a stimulating colour. You probably thought you'd get more work out of me if I sat facing a red wall. It infuriated me even before I met you.'

Zac's smile told her she had been precisely right about the red walls in her office. As an advertising man he knew all about the effect that colour had on people at a subconscious level.

'But the agency has an image to maintain, I suppose.' Cindy was beginning to understand fully only as she spoke. 'Everything there has to be efficient, with-it, even ahead of it! I like your flat. Mind you,' she smiled mischievously, 'this room is a little too masculine for my taste.'

'Naturally. Wait till you see my bedroom.'

'I have no intention of seeing your bedroom . . . Why, is it more feminine?'

'No, you idiot. It's got a red ceiling.' He was so pan-faced she took him seriously for a moment. He sat up and looked at her, curled comfortably in the big armchair with her feet tucked under her. Her shoes had been discarded and she looked very lovely with her unruly hair curling softly around her face, the blondeness of it making a stark contrast where it touched the black blouse at her shoulders.

Zac's eyes moved over her slowly, but this time there was something different about his scrutiny. This time he was looking at her as if she were a woman *because* she was a woman. 'So you had me labelled and filed before you met me?'

'I didn't say that. Don't put words in my mouth.'

'And what would have happened to us if I'd never looked further than my first impression?'

'Just what was your first impression, exactly?'

'You—now hang on a minute,' he grinned, 'I won't tell you the very first thing that went through my mind, not in as many words, anyway! It might offend your genteel——'

'Zac!' Cindy's tone held a note of warning. 'There it is again—your reference to my background. You do resent it, don't you?'

He let out a short, impatient breath. 'Will you get that out of your head? Look, did you resent me because I'm the son of a mid-Wales coalminer?'

'Of course not!' It was a moment before the penny dropped. 'Wait a minute, wait a minute. How could I resent that when I didn't even know about it?'

'Well, you know now. No, it was your attitude——'

'We've been through all that.' She shifted uncomfortably, recalling only too well the way Zac had changed all that.

'At the interview, Cindy. Your insolence infuriated me. You'd taken it for granted you'd got the job. You had the nerve to tell me my reputation had gone ahead of me, and gave me the impression you were merely deigning to stay on.'

'And you didn't think I'd be serious about my work.'

'That was something I had to find out. Everyone responds to a stimulus, Cindy. You don't need to work for financial reasons. Yet you were working. That in itself told me there's something lacking in your life. No, I'll amend that. Having seen how hard you work tells me there's something lacking in your life. Everyone can be provoked into action, as I say. It's a question of finding the right button. In your case it was your pride. I put you through your paces and you hated me for it. In the middle of the interview you switched from wanting the job for the right reasons to wanting it for the wrong reason—because you were too proud to be turned down.'

There was a silence.

It didn't last long and it wasn't an awkward silence. Zac Stone was full of surprises. Cindy was realising that with every passing day. He was absolutely right, of course. In everything he'd said.

'So why did you give me the job?'

'I decided it was worth giving you a try when you gave me your little speech, when I saw you had some spirit. But that spirit needed channelling, shaping to my way of things.'

'You make me sound like a wild horse!' Cindy laughed shortly, but Zac wasn't laughing.

'No—absolutely not. Wild horses have their spirits broken, and that's something I'd never want to do to a person. I know only too well what it's like when someone tries to do that to you. No, your spirit just needed harnessing, redirection so that something positive could be gained with it.'

Cindy thought carefully about that, too. And how well Zac Stone had handled her, brought about the change in her. 'Zac . . . thanks for the rise.'

'You earned it.' He stretched out on the settee again and closed his eyes.

'Do you—do you want me to go?' she asked. 'You seem tired tonight. Or distracted or something.'

For just a moment she saw the deep blue of his eyes as he opened and closed them. 'No, don't go. Believe it or not, I haven't had such an interesting evening in a long time.'

Neither had Cindy. She was longing to ask him about himself, but she was afraid she might spoil things between them. As it was, the atmosphere was good, better than it had ever been. In another sense she was quite happy just to share the silence. She let her eyes trail over him, enjoying his face, the broad expanse of his shoulders, the muscular tautness of his stomach, his hips, his legs. She wanted Zac. There was no point in denying it to herself any longer when the very sight of him was enough to stir an aching response in her, the like of which she had never before experienced in her twenty-three years.

But nothing would come of it. Of that she would

make absolutely certain. She had to. It was a question
of self-preservation: With a man such as he it would
mean——

'Cindy,' he said slowly, 'do you know what the single
biggest troublemaker in the world is?'

'Yes, as a matter of fact I do.' She smiled inwardly.
Zac had not read her mind. Not when his eyes had been
closed, at any rate. He couldn't know her reasons for
saying what she was about to say. And she certainly
had plenty of them. 'The biggest troublemaker in the
world is sex.'

Zac's eyes opened and he smiled wryly. 'No. But that
certainly runs a very close second ... a very close
second. Money is the biggest troublemaker in the
world. Lovely, filthy, lucre.' He punched out the last
three words with equal slowness and stress, and she
wondered once again where he'd been to in his thoughts.

'Zac, can we talk ... about you?'

'My favourite subject.' It was a quip, and it almost
put her off. But not quite.

'You said earlier about my working hard when I
don't need to. You work harder than I do. You push
yourself as I've never seen anyone else do it. Why? You
don't need the money. You're in it for the challenge.
Aren't you?'

When he didn't answer, Cindy regretted having spoken.

After what seemed like a long, long time, he said,
'You're absolutely right—I do it for the challenge. It
hasn't got a damn thing to do with money. Except that
money's inevitable at the end of it. Come over here,
Cindy, I want to kiss you.'

'Zac, please, I'm trying to understand you. You
retired over two years ago. You sold Stone, Mason and
Gibbons after building it from nothing into the top
advertising agency in London. And you'd made
yourself a fortune. You did—well, I don't know what,
for two years——'

'I did nothing. Absolutely nothing ... I've been
wanting to kiss you all evening.'

'It was reported in *Campaign* that you made an agreement in the contract of sale that you'd keep out of advertising completely for one year, so you couldn't set up an agency elsewhere and take the clients with you. But you stayed away for two years. You had no intention of coming back into the rat-race.'

'None whatever,' he said shortly.

'But you did—because there's something missing in your life, too.'

He shifted his large frame lazily, stretched, and then refilled their wineglasses, emptying the bottle. 'Well done! I like a woman who thinks logically.'

He went to the bar and picked up another bottle of wine, opened it and placed it between their glasses. But he didn't sit down again. He moved over to the open windows and looked up at the clear summer sky which had turned into midnight blue. 'I've always been ambitious, Cindy. And I never could resist a challenge. But I regret . . .'

He pushed his hands into his trouser pockets. Cindy said nothing. She just waited, seeing the tension in the muscles of his shoulders.

'. . . I was a born in a small Welsh village. I had three sisters older than myself. My mother worked hard in the home and my father worked down the mines, like his father and his father before him.

'I was brilliant student, with the advantage of an eidetic memory. I won a scholarship to university, and my parents were as proud as punch. They wanted me to go to university as much as I wanted it myself. It was unheard of—a boy in that village in the middle of nowhere who would not be following in his father's footsteps. But I'd never had any intention of doing that; I was born ambitious, and that's something that's stayed with me no matter what I achieved. I wanted to get to the top.

'My parents were religious, and I was brought up accordingly. There were a lot of subjects which were taboo in our house and I was as green as the grass, about many things. Most especially that second biggest troublemaker in the world.'

Zac turned to face her briefly, but he didn't look at her. He was looking beyond her. 'Maybe you're right. Maybe that's the biggest . . . I went through the usual adolescent yearnings and curiosity like anyone else. I did my sexual experimenting with a girl who lived in the next street. She was a pretty girl, cute as anything, and I assumed she was as virginal as I. I was seventeen when we——'

Cindy cringed at the expression he used then, but she made no comment.

'Elisabeth was a year older. Of course she told me she loved me, that that was why she was "allowing" me——'

'She probably did,' Cindy said softly. 'Why do you say it so cynically? She was young, and she——'

'And I was even younger. We only made love once. Just once. And the next thing I knew, she was pregnant. Just that one time, and my entire life——'

'Once is all it takes, Zac.'

'Who are you telling?' he said curtly, bitterly. 'Oh, hell, I'm talking about something that happened twenty years ago; I'm talking about a different era, people—a way of life totally alien to you, Cindy.'

He had his back to her again. His voice quietened so that she had to strain to hear him. 'Life was so cut and dried in those days, in that community. You worked, you worshipped, you lived by the rules. I married Elisabeth—I had no choice. My parents had a fit and so did hers. Her father practically marched me to the altar with the proverbial shotgun. It's a classic, I know, and it happens time and again all over the world.

'So I was married at seventeen and *bang* went my chance at university, my chance of getting out, making money, doing what I wanted to do with my life.'

Cindy looked at him in the ensuing silence, at the expensively furnished flat, at the successful, sophisticated man who stood before her. 'Obviously something

went right for you. What happened? What happened—
about the baby?'

'She miscarried. We were living with her parents,
simply because there was more room in her house. She
was an only child. I was working for a pittance in a
local mill, handing over my wage packet to her mother,
meeting my responsibilities as best I could. I'd grown
up pretty damn quick. But my ambition was burning
more strongly than ever.'

'So when Elisabeth miscarried, you walked out?'

Zac turned and looked at her hard and long. 'You
really don't think much of me, do you?'

'Zac, I'm not judging. I don't think anything. That
wasn't a statement, or an accusation, it was a question.
Did you leave?'

'I left. We *both* left. The reason for my marriage no
longer existed, but I thought we could make it work. I
wanted to make it work. You see, in my own young,
naïve way, I loved her a little.

'But it had to be on my terms from then on. Elisabeth
knew I was ambitious; the entire village knew I'd
planned on going to university. There was no way I'd
have remained poor the rest of my life—with or without
the baby's presence. Once the responsibility of
fatherhood had gone, though, I was obviously able to
move quicker.

'I talked to Elisabeth at length. I was eighteen by
then; she was nineteen. She was against the idea of
leaving Wales, her family, her familiar, safe world. But
she came to London with me.'

'She loved you, Zac. She'd loved you all along.'

'That's what I thought, too. You sound as naïve as I
was in those days. I was a meal ticket to her. *That's*
what I'd been all along. Firstly, she'd needed me to
marry her. Then she discovered life was easier having a
husband. It meant she didn't need to work. She refused
to get a job in London, and you can imagine how broke
we were. I was working in an agency as a mail boy and
messenger. But Elisabeth had been brought up to think

that a woman should be kept—and she never changed those ideas, regardless of how much we needed more money.

'I was fascinated by the big city, mesmerised by the advertising world. I listened, I learned, I picked brains. I was going to make it to the top. I worked long hours and I studied in the evening. I educated myself . . . and all the time, Elisabeth nagged me. To return to Wales, to stop working so hard, to take my head out of my books.

'After eighteen months, the inevitable happened. There was an almighty row—a very, very nasty row. In the midst of it, in her hysteria, she told me the baby she'd been carrying wasn't even mine. Before me, she'd been well and truly initiated by some kid who lived on a farm. He'd enlisted and joined the army before she realised she was pregnant. How I didn't kill Elisabeth that night, I'll never know to this day . . . *Then* I walked out.'

The sudden silence seemed to ring in Cindy's ears. She didn't know what to say, so she said nothing at all.

Zac lifted his glass and smiled at her. 'Admittedly, I envy you your education, Cindy, your opportunities. But I don't resent your background, for the very reason that my own background was against me. When I was working my way through the ranks, I had to compete with university graduates. But I made it regardless.

'So a person's roots, history or whatever we want to call it, never enters into the scheme of things when I hire or fire. I hire if I think they can do the job, I fire if I find I've made a mistake. If they don't like my pace, the way I run things—well, you know the old adage about the heat and the kitchen.'

Cindy nodded, watching him over the rim of her glass. By the time the second bottle of wine was finished it was well into the night. She was drowsy, and it was obvious Zac was tired. But they just went on talking.

Cindy told him something about her own family, but she didn't tell him much about herself. Talking about her innermost thoughts and hopes was something she would find difficult to do with anyone. The dawn chorus had started by the time their conversation went full circle, several cups of coffee and some rather stale sandwiches later.

'So you reached the zenith and then you retired. Why?'

'There was nothing else to do. What was left? I got tired, too. I decided I wanted to use money, that money wasn't going to use me. I bought a house in the Bahamas, just outside Nassau. It's still there; I let friends use it from time to time. I've got friends, contacts all over the world.

'I got bored, Cindy. B-o-r-e-d. You can only do so much jet-setting, attend so many parties, have more affairs than you can remember. And it palls, does it not, eventually?'

'I—suppose so.' She was hardly qualified to comment on those remarks. 'Zac . . . what happened to—to your wife?'

Draining the last of his coffee he looked at her sharply. '*Ex*-wife, if you don't mind. As far as I know she's alive and well and living in Swansea with four kids and a husband. My mother used to give me bulletins from time to time, irrespective of my not wishing to know. She used to hear gossip.'

'Used to?'

A shadow crossed his face then. 'Yes—my mother died three years ago, I'm afraid. My father went about two weeks later. I always knew it would happen like that, when one went the other wouldn't last long. They were devoted to one another.'

Cindy got to her feet and stepped into her shoes, wanting to get away from the subject of his parents. She had obviously touched on a tender spot. 'So you came back again to start from scratch. You don't need the money, but you do need the challenge. That's why you took over Bryant's.'

'Precisely so.' Zac's arms came around her from behind

and she turned slowly to face him, found herself lifting her head to receive his kiss because it seemed like the natural, the only thing to do. Her arms closed around the broadness of his back as if by a will of their own.

His kiss was an exploration, a discovery, and was so sweet in its eroticism that she felt the room shift behind the blackness of her closed eyes. She pulled away from him, her breath catching on words he would not allow her to speak. Again he kissed her, and again it was different.

This time, it was a demand.

It seemed to Cindy that she had no strength at all, that it was Zac's strength, his caresses over her hips, her back, her breasts, that prevented her legs from giving way beneath her. She was pressed tightly against the hardness of his body, her response as immediate as his own, a response she was powerless to withhold. But she must, she *must*. Hadn't he just told her he'd had more affairs than he could remember? Meaningless affairs . . .

She stepped away from him, wishing she could as easily cut herself off from this impossible, impelling attraction she felt for him. 'Zac, I—I don't want things to be like this between us. You're my boss, and that's all I want you to be to me.'

Gently, he tilted her face in his hand. He looked deeply into the darkness of her eyes as if he would read her most private, innermost thoughts. 'Cindy, I know women. Quite apart from all I've told you, it's my business to know women, to know what motivates them, what they want, what they don't want, what they really hope for when they say one thing and mean something else . . .'

She closed her eyes against his words, words spoken very quietly. Dear Lord, he had no right. No right to read her so easily.

'. . . I know when a woman wants me. When the time is right, Cindy, I shall make love to you. And you will welcome it. Now go home, proud beauty, and sleep well.'

CHAPTER SIX

'CINDY, have you dropped off to sleep or something?' Zac's voice boomed at her from the adjoining office. He rarely used the intercom on his desk; it was hardly worth it when his door was always open and he found it easier to shout. 'I asked you to get three phone calls twenty minutes ago—and I'm still waiting! Get on with it. I haven't got all day.'

They didn't have all day. It was almost noon on the Wednesday morning and at lunchtime she and Zac were driving down to Croydon to see a client. 'They're engaged, Zac.'

'What? All of them?'

'Yes.' Cindy refused to get flustered. The pressure was on more than ever because the presentation of the new campaign for Simpson's was due to be held on the following Monday. Everyone was working flat out.

She closed her eyes briefly as Zac shouted at her to keep trying the calls. As if she wouldn't! She wondered what on earth was upsetting him; he wasn't usually this bad. He'd been all right until about half an hour ago . . .

'And get Sheila in here in the meantime,' he went on. 'Like now!'

Cindy buzzed Sheila and passed on the message. But when she switched to an outside line in order to try the calls again, Twin-Set and Pearls came bursting into the office. She was obviously upset, even close to tears.

Cindy looked at her in amazement. She'd never seen Miss Druce like this before. 'What is it, Miss Druce? What's happened?' She put down the phone at once.

'I'd like to see Mr Stone.' There was a stubborn look on Miss Druce's face.

'Miss Druce, can't you tell me?' Cindy lowered her voice, 'Zac's awfully busy. I don't want to disturb him.' It wasn't only that, actually. The mood Zac was in was not a good one, and he wouldn't want to be bothered with——

'Neither do I.' Miss Druce stood erect, immovable. 'But this is very important!' Her voice rose. 'I must see Mr Stone. Now!'

Zac appeared in the doorway, frowning. 'Miss Druce, come in. Come in, my dear.'

He ushered Twin-Set and Pearls into his office and closed the door behind them. Alison and Cindy exchanged questioning looks, but there was no time to speculate as to what ailed Miss Druce. Alison didn't even stop typing. She was working as hard as Cindy these days, though at least she finished on time.

'What does he want now?' Sheila came in looking positively hung-over. She was wearing red and black striped jeans and a yellow tee-shirt and she looked like nothing on earth.

'Got a hangover, Sheila?' Alison had obviously had the same thought as Cindy.

'Less of the lip—this is overwork.' She turned to Cindy. 'I'll go in, then. Granite Face has summoned, and I must come running.'

'Hold it!' Cindy leapt from her chair and put a restraining hand on Sheila's arm. Sheila was cross with Zac because he'd rejected two lots of copy she'd written of late. 'Miss Druce is in there. Just wait a couple of minutes, would you?'

Sheila waited five minutes. She flopped into a chair and stuck her feet on the radiator. There wasn't a sound coming from Zac's office and Sheila looked at her watch every sixty seconds. 'Right! I'm off! Buzz me again when those two have finished——'

Sheila broke off as the adjoining door opened and Miss Druce came sailing out of Zac's office with a satisfied look on her face. As the door closed behind her, Sheila got to her feet just as Zac yelled to Cindy. 'So where the hell is Sheila?'

'Here, Zac, here!'

Sheila flounced in cockily, not bothering to close the door behind her. 'You sent for me?' she said sweetly, her voice dripping with sarcasm.

'Sit down, Sheila.' Zac's voice was curt, impatient.

'I would if your chairs weren't covered with a pile of junk.'

Alison and Cindy exchanged looks again. There had been a storm brewing between Zac and Sheila for over a week—it seemed it was about to break.

'Stand, then!' Zac shouted. 'For heaven's sake, what are you wearing? You look bloody awful. Don't stand on those papers, you idiot!'

There was a moment's silence, then a rustle of papers.

'Sheila, how long have you worked at Bryant's?'

'Ten years.'

'And how long have you been writing copy for the Eleanor account?'

'Five years,' Sheila's voice was both sullen and defiant. 'Since they first came to us.'

'I've just read your latest attempt on the copy that's supposed to go with the new photographs—you are aware that we've got a deadline on this?'

'Oh, for God's sake! Don't tell me you're still not satisfied?' Sheila was shouting now, and Zac shouted back at her with equal force.

'Satisfied? It's tripe! Just like your previous attempts. It's stale, clichéd and boring. *You're* stale, Sheila. You've dried up!'

'The hell I've dried up! How many ways are there to describe women's underwear?'

'An infinite number!' Zac boomed. 'Look at this. Read it! You've merely described that bra, right down to its last piece of lace. We've got the photographs to do that for us! Wait a minute, wait a minute . . .'

There was the sound of Zac striding angrily around his office, the rustle of tissue paper and then the command, 'Catch! Now get yourself into the ladies' room and pour yourself into that.'

At that point, Alison cracked up with laughter and Cindy shot her a warning look. True, Sheila would never be able to 'pour' herself into anything. She was as thin as a rake and she never even wore a bra.

The row flared. It was like a ping-pong match, Sheila giving as good as she got and Zac beating her down. 'We're not aiming at middle-aged ladies, we're aiming at the very young with this lot!' Zac went on. 'You haven't read the market research, have you?'

'Of course I've read the research! Of course I'm aware of the market!'

'Well, it doesn't show, lady. It doesn't show. Take these, too. And this. Go and put them on and *feel* what the garments are like next to your skin. *Feel* how comfortable they are, how natural. They're delicious, Sheila. Delicious! That's what I want you to write about. Let your imagination run away with you! Tell the readers why it's worth spending extra money on Eleanor underwear instead of buying stuff from a chain store. Tell them what it's going to do to their husbands or boy-friends when they wear these silky, seductive things. Tell them how good their figures are going to look, how this stuff is going to flatter the line of their clothes. *That's* what women are interested in. You're not writing about Simpson's furniture here, you know, you're writing about *seduction*! If you can't come up with something original next time, I'm taking you off the account!'

Sheila, tight-faced, white-faced, slammed out of Zac's office with a pair of French knickers in her hand and two bras slung over her shoulder. She was cursing generally and Zac in particular as she slammed the door to Cindy's office, too.

Alison, who had been almost prostrate throughout all this, made an effort to calm herself when she saw that Cindy wasn't in the least amused. 'I wonder why he talks to Sheila like that? You don't think he'll fire her, do you?'

'No.' Cindy sighed and started dialling again. 'He's just pressing the right button.'

'What?'

'Oh, it doesn't matter, Alison. I was just thinking aloud. He won't fire Sheila, don't worry.'

'It's strange, really, because he's always so nice to me.'

'Yes.' Cindy smiled, put the call through to Zac, and nipped out for a sandwich while she had the chance.

It was turned nine o'clock when they left Croydon that evening. Zac had invited his client to dinner when the meeting finally broke up at a little after six, and the three of them had gone on talking shop through the meal.

After she'd been in Zac's car for a few minutes, Cindy's eyes closed. She was tired, but she wasn't in danger of actually falling asleep. She was thinking about the man beside her.

She had seen Zac Stone when he was with clients, at his most charming. She had watched him relating to his staff, his team, motivating them to produce their best work and knowing precisely how to do that, according to their personalities. And in his home last week she had learned what motivated Zac. Had she seen, then, a glimpse of the real man?

But one couldn't really separate Zac's personality into compartments. The different facets of him were inextricably intertwined. One could only look at the whole, because sometimes he behaved in the most unpredictable way. Like this afternoon, for example, when at one point he'd been downright rude to his client. But he had done it in such a way that the man had taken it; had been unable to argue with the point Zac had made. Then there had been that other unpredictable moment during the morning, when he had taken time out of his busy schedule to placate Miss Druce over whatever it was that ailed her.

As much as Cindy had learned about him, Zac was still very much a mystery to her. On a person-to-person basis she trusted him, instinctively, even though she was well aware that he was a manipulator of people. Conversely, on a man-woman basis, she didn't trust him an inch! All she could really be certain of, absolutely certain, was that Zac Stone was a winner, a man who got what he wanted.

'Penny for your thoughts?'

Cindy didn't open her eyes. The very nearness of him, the fact that they were alone in his car, affected her. She didn't want to open her eyes and complicate her thoughts even further by looking at him. 'They're not worth it,' she said casually. 'They're illogical, jumbled.'

'That doesn't sound like you.' Cindy sensed, rather than saw, the look he gave her. He said nothing else. He turned the car radio on very low and they drove in silence.

He was right, too. It wasn't like Cindy. It wasn't like her to tie herself up in knots, to be so indecisive over what she felt for someone. Man or woman, she was usually quick to make up her mind about people. But most especially about men.

She had stopped disliking Zac, but what exactly did she feel for him—now? Fascination? Admiration? Respect?

She did look at him then. She opened her eyes slightly and watched him from beneath lowered lashes. The lights from the oncoming traffic were flickering across his strong, dark features, making him look more mysterious than ever.

Desire. Yes, there was that, too. And because of that she felt an element of resentment towards him. She desired Zac Stone, and she resented him because he knew how she felt. And Zac had made it plain what his intentions were as far as that was concerned. Very plain indeed.

Cindy fell asleep then, but before doing so she managed to reach at least one conclusion: there was no way Zac Stone was going to make love to her. For him, it would be sex and nothing else. He had already admitted to having more affairs than he could remember. Well, that was not for Cindy. She wasn't going to number among his conquests!

But it was there, again, as soon as the car engine and the radio were switched off. Cindy opened her eyes to find Zac looking at her, the message in his eyes unmistakable. She had to face it, it was there all the time, crackling between them like electricity. No matter where they were or what they were doing, it was there.

'You know,' he said quietly, 'it can be quite a distraction to a man, having a brown-eyed blonde for a secretary. A beautiful, slender girl who looks like an angel when she's asleep. I don't make a habit of making love to my secretaries, you know. I don't usually go in for office romances.'

Cindy was half-drugged from sleep, but she tried to make her voice as crisp as possible. 'Then I suggest you don't try to break your habit now. And please note—I *never* go in for office romances.'

He laughed at her as she flung open the car door. 'I'll see you in the morning, Goldilocks.'

'Aren't you coming in?'

' 'Fraid not. I've still got a few things to do in the office . . . Unless that was an invitation?'

'It was not an invitation, and you know it. Goodnight, Zac.'

'Well?' Sheila looked at Zac and Cindy looked at Sheila, and held her breath. It was Friday night. It was dark outside. And tempers were raw because everyone was tired.

Zac looked up from the papers Sheila had handed to him and a delighted smile broke out on his face. 'Sheila, you're beautiful! Well, let me not get carried away— your work's beautiful.'

'Satisfied?' She ignored his remark.

'More than.'

'Right,' Sheila nodded. 'Then I'm off. I'm in desperate need of a drink.'

Zac smiled his most charming smile and Sheila looked at him warily. 'Cindy and I are joining Greg and several others in the wine bar. Come with us.'

'Are you buying?'

'I'm buying.'

'Give me two minutes.' Sheila headed for the door. 'You can buy me supper, too.'

Cindy sat back, relieved that things were on an even keel again. She picked up her notebook and stuffed it into her handbag. If several of them were transferring to the wine bar it meant that work wasn't over for the night. They'd all, inevitably, continue to talk shop. Inevitably, because the presentation for Simpson's was due to take place first thing Monday morning. And poor Sheila had had that to cope with as well as the desperately-needed Eleanor copy.

'Supper?' Zac shook his head despairingly. 'You really push your luck, don't you?'

'Always,' Sheila quipped. With an exaggerated toss of her head, she flounced out, to the sound of Zac's laughter.

Cindy stood up and stretched languorously. 'Zac, do you need me? In the wine bar?'

'I need you.' He slapped his hand against the papers he was holding. 'She's good, you know. Damn good . . . Why, are you eager to get off, Cindy? Have you got a late date or something?'

She didn't even bother to answer that one. She'd forgotten what a date was. She hadn't really expected to escape the next hour or so. Oh, but she was tired!

'I warned you,' Zac shrugged, 'what it would be like when the pressure's on. Working half the night, over the weekends. I hope you didn't have other plans for this weekend?'

'No. And yes, you warned me, Zac. I don't mind working this weekend, or working half the night. I know it has to be done. It's just that I'd like to have time to go shopping, to have my hair done. . . . Maybe I can have a day off after the presentation? What about Tuesday?'

'No chance. We're going to Paris on Tuesday.' He picked up his jacket and ushered her out of the door.

'Paris?'

'Yes. I've finally succeeded in reaching that chap I wanted a meeting with. We're flying to Paris at lunchtime on Tuesday. We'll be wining and dining him in the evening, and the meeting with his Board will take place on Wednesday morning. So brush up your French.'

Just like that! No warning, no explanation!

'Zac, you haven't told me what this is all about yet! Who are we going to see? And why? And how long will we be there? And what about air tickets and accommodation?'

'I've arranged our rooms and our flights.' He switched off the lights in his office and hooked his jacket over his shoulder. 'We'll be there two nights, maybe three. As for your other questions, I'll brief you some time before we leave.'

Cindy glanced at him curiously as they met up with Sheila. She asked no more questions, but she could tell from the light in Zac's eyes that their trip to Paris was very, very important to him.

To all intents and purposes, Saturday was just another day at work. It was typically hectic and fraught. Most of the creative people were working over the weekend, two other secretaries were in, half the art department and, of course, Greg Halliday, who was actually in charge of the Simpson account. Greg and Zac worked incredibly well together. As Creative Director, Zac had spent a great deal of time with Greg deciding on their plans in the early stages of the proposed campaign and between the two men, interestingly enough, there was never a raised voice, never an angry word.

It was exciting to see it all coming together. Cindy's mind went back to the day when the idea had been sold to Simpson's, then forward to the day when she'd see the advertisements on the television. It was an exciting process, an exciting world.

But in spite of that she was still waiting for things to level off a little. The pressure was catching up with her, and there were moments when she did ask herself quite why it was that she pushed herself so hard these days.

Maybe Zac saw her exhaustion. Or maybe he, too, was feeling it. Whatever, he came into Cindy's office in the latter half of Sunday afternoon and told her to go home.

'Are you calling it a day, Zac?'

'I can't.' He leaned against the door jamb and looked at his watch. 'I've got a couple of other matters to talk over with Greg. But you don't need to be there, Cindy. Go home and take a nap. I'm taking you out to dinner this evening, okay?'

'Okay.' Cindy smiled at him. This was Zac's way of rewarding her hard work.

'Wear something sensational,' he called to her as she was leaving the room. 'I'll pick you up at eight.'

CHAPTER SEVEN

'ZAC, however did you find this place? I've driven past it several times and I didn't even realise it was a restaurant. I mean, there's no sign outside. There's just a small brass plate and a rather discreet front door!' Cindy laughed. 'I really like it. It's got such ... such atmosphere.'

They were sipping pre-dinner drinks, their second pre-dinner drinks. They had spent half an hour chatting over a drink in Cindy's flat after Zac had called for her. After a two-hour nap and a leisurely bath, Cindy was feeling refreshed and relaxed. She was looking her best, with her hair swept up on the crown of her head, a few wispy curls left loose to add softness to the style.

Her dress was classic, simple, made from a soft, clingy material the colour of ivory. Around the low neckline and back there was a single twist of gold thread running through the material. She would hardly call it sensational, but she knew she looked good in it.

Zac seemed pleased by her remark. 'I was one of their first customers when they opened about seven years ago. The chap who showed us to the table is new, but the owner's an old friend of mine. He runs the kitchen himself and he's an artist. Wait till you taste the food and you'll see what I mean.'

Zac had ordered for her. He seemed to know just what she liked, and the food lived up to his recommendation. They drank too much wine, which didn't matter because they hadn't brought the car with them, and Cindy grew more mellow and relaxed as the evening went on.

'Tell me, how ambitious are you, Cindy? Have you set your sights on a Directorship at Bryant's? Or are

LOVE BEYOND REASON
There was a surprise in store for Amy!

Amy had thought nothing could be as perfect as the days she had shared with Vic Hoyt in New York City—before he took off for his Peace Corps assignment in Kenya.

Impulsively, Amy decided to follow. She was shocked to find Vic established in his new life... and interested in a new girl friend.

Amy faced a choice: be smart and go home... or stay and fight for the only man she would ever love.

MAN OF POWER
Sara took her role seriously

Although Sara had already planned her escape from the subservient position in which her father's death had placed her, Morgan Haldane's timely appearance had definitely made it easier.

All Morgan had asked in return was that she pose as his fiancée. He'd confessed to needing protection from his partner's wife, Louise, and the part of Sara's job proved easy.

But unfortunately for Sara's heart, Morgan hadn't told her about Monique...

Your Romantic Adventure Starts Here.

THE LEO MAN
"He's every bit as sexy as his father!"

Her grandmother thought that description would appeal to Rowan, but Rowan was determined to avoid any friendship with the arrogant James Fraser.

Aboard his luxury yacht, that wasn't easy. When they were all shipwrecked on a tropical island, it proved impossible.

And besides, if it weren't for James, none of them would be alive. Rowan was confused. Was it merely gratitude that she now felt for this strong and rugged man?

THE WINDS OF WINTER
She'd had so much— now she had nothing

Anne didn't dwell on it, but the pain was still with her—the double-edged pain of grief and rejection.

It had greatly altered her; Anne barely resembled the girl who four years earlier had left her husband, David. He probably wouldn't even recognize her—especially with another name.

Anne made up her mind. She just had to go to his house to discover if what she suspected was true...

These FOUR free Harlequin Romance novels allow you to enter the world of romance, love and desire. As a member of the Harlequin Home Subscription Plan, you can continue to experience all the moods of love. You'll be inspired by moments so real. . .so moving. . .you won't want them to end. So start your own Harlequin Romance adventure by returning the reply card below. <u>DO IT TODAY!</u>

EXTRA BONUS
MAIL YOUR ORDER
TODAY AND GET A
FREE TOTE BAG
FROM HARLEQUIN.

you planning to give it all up in a couple of years and settle down to marriage and a dozen children?'

'Neither!' She giggled at the two extremes of his questions. 'I wouldn't want a Directorship. I'm not that ambitious! All I want really was to succeed at something. If I'm doing that as secretary to the most demanding man in advertising, then I'm satisfied.'

'You are.' Zac smiled at the way she'd referred to him, his deep blue eyes intense and very beautiful in the muted lighting. 'I love it when you laugh like that,' he added quietly, 'and may I say you're looking incredibly beautiful this evening . . . But let me not digress! Why was it so important to you to succeed at something?'

Cindy didn't need to think about that. 'I suppose my family's partly the reason for that. In my teens and as a child there were so many things I wasn't allowed to do because I was the daughter of Sir Robert Hetherington, Q.C., a man who was very much in the public eye in those days.' She broke off, hearing the cynicism in her own voice. 'It . . . was the same for all of us, of course. I have two sisters older than myself. And I was never any good at anything. Oh, I was bright enough in school, but that was only because I was sent to the best places and they taught me well. I was a very unattractive little girl . . .'

'I find that hard to believe.'

Cindy bowed her head graciously. 'It's true. I was grossly overweight in my early teens, which in turn made me shy and lacking in confidence, and I had a chip on my shoulder about it. I came to London when I was nineteen, after a year doing virtually nothing at home. I wanted to live by myself, get away from the family's clutches, sort of thing. I wanted an identity of my own.'

Zac laughed quietly. 'And you wanted to have some fun. You still had that to get out of your system. You were young and beautiful by then, I take it.'

'I don't know about that.' Cindy was giggling again.

One part of her mind was telling her she'd drunk too much wine, that she was talking too much, and at the same time she didn't really care. She didn't mind telling Zac about herself now. And he was so easy to talk to . . . 'I was young, yes. And I was slim!'

'So you tried your wings.'

'I started work at Bryant's when I was nineteen. But my evenings in those days were very different from my current evenings! I lived in Hampstead then, with a couple of other girls. We all had fun—dinners, dates, dancing, seeing the clubs and so on. We all went our separate ways within a couple of years. When I was twenty-one I inherited the money my grandmother left me—please note, my *grandmother*. My father does not keep me in the lap of luxury, as you once called it. I took the flat in Priory Court and, frankly, I like living alone. The idea of living it up these days doesn't appeal to me in the least.'

'That makes sense,' Zac shrugged. 'You got it out of your system.'

'It palled, Zac. Just as you were saying, about your retirement. I got b-o-r-e-d with it. I concentrated fully on my job from then on, working for the M.D. and all that. But it's only now that I'm getting real satisfaction from my work. I've got this *dreadful* boss, you see . . .'

'Out of order!' Zac summoned the waiter and looked at Cindy in mock disdain. 'You were making so much sense till you came out with that remark! Come on, I think you need a little fresh air.'

'But Zac,' she said innocently, 'if the wine's loosened my tongue a little—well, alcohol brings out the truth, doesn't it?'

They were delayed from leaving when a tall, thin man—made even taller by the chef's hat he wore—emerged from the kitchen and made a beeline for their table.

'Zac! It's wonderful to see you. When I saw your name in the bookings for this evening—well, I was amazed. I thought we'd lost you for ever to the

Bahamas.' He bowed graciously as Zac introduced him to Cindy.

'Paul Denning, Cindy Hetherington. Congratulations on the dinner, Paul. You haven't lost your touch.'

'It was superb,' Cindy added.

Paul took hold of her hand and kissed the back of it, his eyes sweeping over her appreciatively. 'You and Zac will be regulars from now on. Zac always used to be, you know. When did you get back to England, Zac?'

'Several weeks ago.'

The owner of the restaurant looked mortally wounded. 'Several weeks—and I see nothing of you till tonight?'

'I've been busy,' Zac laughed. 'I've taken over Bryant's.'

'Indeed? I hadn't heard . . . And why? I thought you were sick of the advertising world?'

Zac waved a dismissive arm. 'Some other time, Paul. That's another story.'

Before moving off to the next table, Paul invited them to join him and some other friends at a private dinner party he was giving one night the following week, when the restaurant was closed.

'Sorry.' Zac shrugged apologetically. 'We'd have loved to, but we're going to Paris on Tuesday.'

Paul smiled rather wistfully, his eyes moving over Cindy once more. 'Well, give Paris my regards.'

Zac laughed shortly as Paul moved on. 'He must think we're going on some sort of pleasure trip.'

'Evidently,' Cindy said quietly. 'You might have introduced me as your secretary. I'm sure he thinks I'm your mistress or something.'

'Would that be such a bad thing?'

'A very bad thing.'

He put a hand under her arm as they left, whispering in her ear, 'I thought alcohol made people tell the truth.'

'It does.'

They walked home slowly, Cindy's arm linked

through Zac's. It was a beautifully warm August evening and she was heady from the wine, the superb dinner—Zac's nearness. He was looking very attractive in a light grey suit and a crisp white shirt, and the moment they stepped out of the restaurant, he loosened his tie. Cindy smiled inwardly; she could have predicted that. Even on cool days Zac tugged impatiently as his tie the instant he no longer needed to be concerned about his appearance.

'How's your mother?'

'What?' After a lengthy silence Zac's question came as a surprise. 'My mother? She's fine. I spent an hour chatting to her on the phone this afternoon. In fact, the phone was ringing when I got in. Mummy's like that. She'd spend all day chatting to me on the phone!'

'And your father, what does he think of you working in advertising?'

'I haven't the faintest idea what my father thinks——' Cindy stopped short. Zac Stone really had the cleverest way of drawing her out. The funny thing was that she didn't mind. And that wasn't due to the wine; the fresh air was rapidly clearing her head.

Zac motioned her towards a bench on a small green patch in front of a building. 'It's always "Mummy" and "my father". Every time you speak of him there's bitterness in your voice. It worries me, Cindy. What happened between you two that's made you feel like this?'

'God, you're nosey! Don't you know enough about me yet? Even now?'

'No.'

Cindy let out a long breath. 'All right. When I was thirteen I walked in on my father when he was . . . being unfaithful to my mother.' She could hardly believe her own ears. She'd never told that to anyone.

Zac made a clicking sound with his tongue. 'That was unfortunate.'

'Unfortunate? Unfortunate! For whom?'

'For all concerned. For you, at that age. For your

father, who'll never forget it. For the woman, who was embarrassed. What happened?'

Cindy looked at him quickly, wondering how he could be so damned nonchalant about it. 'I-it was with a house guest. Well, a sort of au pair, I suppose. She was Swiss, in her twenties, the daughter of a family my parents knew in Zurich. She'd been living in our house for about three weeks when . . . You don't want the gory details.'

'Oh, but I do. Go on.' He wasn't smiling. At least he wasn't amused.

'I was a weekly boarder in those days. I came home every weekend. My father and I were pals. As hard as he worked, he still tried hard to be the family man. He didn't mind that I was fat. I was Daddy's little girl . . . my sisters were in their early twenties when I was thirteen. They never found out about this . . .

'Anyway, I was home for the summer holidays and one night there was a terrifying storm—I've always been terrified of storms. I was crying. I couldn't cope on my own and I bolted for the nearest bedroom . . . Anna's. And there they were. There was no lock on the door, and there they were. The so-called pillar of the community, the highly respectable Sir Robert, and his au pair. I'll never forget that moment. The shock of it. The lights were on, the bedclothes were off and I burst in on them while they were actually, actually——'

Zac finished the sentence for her and Cindy looked down at the grass. 'Zac, must you be so graphic?'

He shrugged carelessly. 'Would it be fairer to describe it as lovemaking, when there's all the difference in the world between that and lovemaking? It was just sex, wasn't it? Your parents sound happy enough together now. Or was there a string of others after Anna?'

'I—no. Not to my knowledge.' Cindy was getting irritated. Just sex? Oh, where had she heard that before?

'And your mother? Did you tell her or did your father?'

Cindy got up and started walking again. 'Firstly, Anna left the following morning. Secondly, I suppose my father must have told my mother, because I refused to go downstairs the following morning. I'd cried all night, and was still crying when Mummy came to me. But she knew in any case.'

At that, Zac's eyebrows rose slightly.

Cindy shrugged. In for a penny . . . 'My mother had had a hysterectomy. Prior to that she'd had a lot of menopausal trouble. Unlike you, Zac, I wasn't green about these things at thirteen. I understood it all, intellectually. My mother is a lady in every sense of the word. She explained to me that she hadn't given my father any "attention" in a long time. She said I should try to understand that this wasn't serious, that my father still loved her, and I should forgive him.'

'And you never have.'

'Zac, I find the whole thing very distasteful.' Cindy snapped. 'I don't want to discuss it any further. My father and I have never really communicated since that day. There's a strain between us and—well, it'll always be there.'

'That's a shame, my beauty.' Zac looked at her curiously then. 'It was one of those things. Your father fell from grace because you found out he was human.'

He held open the door for her as they entered Priory Court, bade the doorman good evening and punched the lift button.

In a quiet, tight voice, Cindy contradicted him. 'I found out he was a hypocrite. I found out he was *unfaithful*.'

'To whom?'

She stepped into the lift, glaring at him. 'To my mother, of course.'

'But she forgave him. Why couldn't you? Your father was only unfaithful to your image of him. It's always a blow when we discover that our parents are only human, with human susceptibilities. You're a big girl now, Cindy. It's about time you stopped thinking about all this in the way you thought about it ten years ago . . . Put the kettle on, would you? I want to talk to you about Paris.'

She had followed Zac into his flat without even stopping to think about it. In fact, it was minutes later before she realised she'd walked into a potentially dangerous situation. For the moment she was too busy thinking about what he'd said. Never once in ten years had she stopped to think what it must have been like from her father's point of view, how he must have felt when she had walked in on him. 'Your father fell from grace because you found out he was human . . .' But wasn't that typical of a man, to take it lightly, to put it down as being 'just sex'?

Cindy carried the coffee into the living room in a state of agitation. What was she doing here? She'd had no intention whatever of ending the evening in Zac's flat . . .

'Paris,' he said crisply. 'Sorry to end this evening with business, Cindy, but we'll have no opportunity tomorrow.'

'That's all right.' She relaxed slightly and poured the coffee. It was impossible to think about three things at once, despite the training Zac had given her! She would think about her father some other time. She would keep her guard up until she left Zac's flat and try to concentrate fully on what he was saying.

'You remember the man at the party?'

'The perfume manufacturer, yes. His agency were ditching him because they were going after bigger business in the same line.'

'Germaine Perfumes,' Zac nodded. 'Very big business.'

'I wear Germaine perfumes occasionally. I shouldn't have thought they were that big. They do a small but very exclusive range of——' Cindy stopped dead. Germaine Perfumes were based in Paris.

'They're launching a new range—mass market, medium price. They've got a three-quarter-of-a-million-pound budget. All that lovely lolly to spend on their launch! And you know how much profit that will mean to the agency who gets it. The follow-up business will be big, too.' Zac rubbed his hand across the back of his neck, easing the tension from his shoulders.

Cindy laughed excitedly. 'Now I understand why you refused the little man's business. *We're* pitching for Germaine's!'

'Don't get excited. I'm superstitious. I've told you before, I might count my chickens before they're hatched, but I don't like talking about it.'

'But Zac, need you worry? With your reputation and——'

He held up a silencing hand. 'There are three other agencies pitching for the business.'

'Mm. Well, that's normal . . .'

'Including Cookson Associates.'

Cindy flinched. Cooksons were good. 'Ouch.'

'And there's something else.' Zac drained his coffee and stretched out on the settee. 'Our three competitors are preparing speculative campaigns. They were given the go-ahead eight weeks ago.'

Cindy had to make an effort not to leap up from her chair. '*Eight weeks ago?* Why, you hadn't even taken over Bryant's then! We've got no chance of preparing a campaign in time! Zac, what you're telling me is that we're too late. Germaine Perfumes don't even want a fourth agency to pitch for the business, do they?'

'No.'

'How come we didn't learn about this sooner? Well, I mean you weren't even around when these other agencies——'

Zac waved an arm at her. 'It makes no difference. The whole business has been kept under wraps because it's the launch of a new product. The chap at the party told me about it because he's disgruntled.'

Cindy was shaking her head. 'And how did you manage to get an arrangement to see the Board of Germaine's?'

'I know the Chairman. Is there any more coffee in the pot?'

'Sorry. I only made two cups. Zac, please, what did the Chairman say?'

'A lot of things. It took me almost an hour to talk him into arranging the meeting.'

'So he's doing you a favour, letting you talk to his Board. What else did he say?'

'He said I'll never talk them into it. They're not interested. He said I was crazy.' Zac closed his eyes. 'Are you making more coffee?'

'In a minute. You know what I think?'

'What?'

'I think you're crazy!' Cindy got to her feet, shaking her head. There were three competing agencies preparing speculative campaigns and they'd had eight weeks in which to make their preparations. Zac had been told by the Chairman of Germaine Perfumes that they weren't interested in letting another agency prepare a campaign. Apart from that, they were too late! Why was he bothering to waste money on plane fares?

Zac was sound asleep when she went in with the coffee. It shouldn't have surprised her, considering the way he'd been working, but it did.

Cindy put the coffee down and just stood, watching him as he slept. What a strange man he was—unshockable and shocking, predictable and unpredictable, brilliant, and crazy with it. She stood for minutes, just looking at him. How often he gave her food for thought. Tonight he'd given her a feast!

She picked up her bag and left the flat very, very quietly. Looking at Zac, she had suddenly been filled with a strange, unaccountable sadness. For one awful moment, she'd imagined she was beginning to fall in love with him.

She shook herself mentally as she closed her own front door.

She was probably just tired.

CHAPTER EIGHT

PARIS was shrouded in grey clouds. There was a fine, misty drizzle falling, the type of rain that is far more unpleasant than a torrent.

Cindy and her boss emerged from the airport two hours later than planned, owing to a delay in take-off at London's Heathrow.

'Not to worry.' Zac ushered her into a taxi and told the driver to take them to the Hotel George V. 'Alain is coming to the hotel at seven. We've got plenty of time.'

Cindy hardly heard him. 'The George Cinq? Oh, why didn't you tell me we were staying there?' She was excited. 'I've always wanted to!'

'You didn't ask.' Zac smiled at the look on her face. 'You mean you've never seen the place?'

'Never.' The famous hotel was old and very majestic. It had been patronised over the years by maharajahs and millionaires, by Royalty and film stars. 'I've only been to Paris once before, for three days. It was a school trip.' Cindy pulled a face at the memory. 'So you can imagine the sights we took in—the museums, art galleries, Notre Dame, the Sacré Coeur. Oh, it was interesting, but we didn't exactly get the flavour of Paris, didn't see anything romantic!'

Zac was laughing now. 'But you spent a year in France with friends of your family. Didn't they bring you to Paris?'

'Paris was hardly local to where I was staying! Besides, I wasn't old enough to see any night life. I mean, places like the Moulin Rouge and the——'

'Hold it!' Zac's eyes were lit with amusement. 'We're on a business trip, remember?' He took hold of her hand and moved a little closer to her. 'But we'll have one spare evening. I'll see what I can do . . .'

Cindy turned to look out of the window. In a way, she was sorry she'd spoken. What she'd said could very easily be misunderstood. She didn't worry about what the rain would do to her hair. She watched the passing scenery in a state of fascination. Some people were hurrying along, some were strolling, some were sitting under the umbrellas of pavement cafés regardless of the weather. Everything in Paris was said to start at café tables, from business deals to romance.

Cindy's eyes flitted about eagerly, from the top of the Eiffel Tower to the windows of the buildings in which the Parisians were going about their daily business. She looked longingly at the smart shops on the Champs-Elysées, wishing she had time to do more than just look. How different Paris seemed now from the way it had seemed when she was a schoolgirl. She saw it now as it really was—exciting, romantic, mysterious, cosmopolitan, utterly fascinating.

Just below the Arc de Triomphe the driver turned into the Avenue Georges V. The foyer of the hotel was more like the hallway of a stately home. It was magnificent, with a beautiful, pinkish Aubusson carpet which must have cost a fortune. The receptionist, immaculately clad, stood behind what could only be described as a very discreet little desk, no more than three or four feet wide.

They were greeted and treated with the utmost courtesy and a uniformed porter appeared as if from nowhere to show them to their rooms . . .

Except that they weren't staying in rooms. They were staying in a suite which comprised two bedrooms, with a bathroom between, and a very elegant sitting room. The suite was beautiful, but Cindy hadn't anticipated . . . 'I—I had no idea we'd be staying in the same suite, Zac.' She turned to him as soon as the porter left.

'I can't talk to my secretary if she's staying on the other side of the hotel, can I?' Zac tugged at his tie and dropped his jacket over the arm of a chair. Then he looked at her, as if he'd only just caught the implications. 'Hey, relax, will you?' He smiled roguishly. 'After all, you have got your own bedroom!'

'I hope the door's got a lock on it.' Cindy did not smile back.

Zac picked up the telephone. 'Why don't you go and investigate while I order coffee?' He looked at his watch. 'Would you like something to eat?'

'No. It's too near dinner time.'

'I'll order you a sandwich. Alain's coming at seven, but knowing him we'll spend at least two hours in the bar before we go in to dinner.'

'Are we dining in the hotel?'

Zac nodded as he gave his order to room service.

Cindy retreated to her bedroom. She'd had no idea Zac spoke a little French. Before doing anything else she checked the door. It had a very ornate gold handle, a sort of lever affair. Of course it was lockable. Cindy laughed at herself. But it was a nervous little laugh. She was not thrilled at the idea of sharing rooms with Zac. It was too intimate for her liking. And the bathroom was situated between their bedrooms, no doubt lockable from both sides . . .

She didn't investigate that. She was too concerned about getting her clothes out of her case and on to hangers. It seemed to Cindy that they'd come to Paris on a hopeless mission, but she would play her role to the best of her ability—which included being suitably dressed for dinner in the hotel with the Chairman of Germaine Perfumes.

The restaurant in the George V was famous for its superb cuisine and though there were countless renowned eating places in Paris, Cindy was delighted she would have the experience of dining at one of the most famous.

She looked round her bedroom with a little smile playing on her lips. The bed was vast, probably the biggest she'd ever seen. In one corner there was a cabinet which turned out to be a fridge. It was stacked with spirits in miniature bottles, and mixers of every description. She dreaded to think what a can of cola would cost in this place, let alone dinner for three in the restuarant. Zac Stone certainly liked the best in life!

The wardrobes were not immediately apparent. They were on either side of the panelled door which led to the bathroom. They were in what had at first glance appeared to be a mirrored wall, but the wall had handles and was in fact a series of doors. A laugh escaped from Cindy at the sheer depth of the wardrobes. She had literally to walk inside in order to hang her clothes!

She heard the arrival of the coffee as she took the last item from her case and joined Zac in the sitting room, still giggling about the size of the wardrobes.

'My dresses look absolutely lost in there!' Cindy laughed as she made herself comfortable in an armchair, her eyes sweeping appreciatively round the room. 'Now *this* is the lap of luxury!'

She poured the coffee and helped herself to a few dainty, prettily presented sandwiches, grateful they had at least a little time in which they could relax.

After recovering from their journey they were faced with a decision. 'Who's having the bathroom first?' Zac took a coin from his pocket and invited Cindy to call.

'Tails—never fails.'

Poker-faced, Zac told her it had this time.

'Let me see . . . you rogue! I win. See you later.'

The bathroom was the size of any ordinary hotel room. Discovering its eccentricities, from the glug-glug of the old-fashioned, ornate taps to the most unusual white porcelain loo which had a blue pattern on it, was an adventure in itself. The loo was tucked away discreetly behind its own little door!

Cindy was still soaking in the bath when Zac called to her. She had taken the precaution of locking the bathroom doors—from each bedroom.

'How long are you going to be in there?'

She was putting the finishing touches to her make-up

when he called again. The light was better in the
bathroom, and she really hadn't taken long.

'For heaven's sake, Cindy! Time's marching on!'

She pulled her gown more closely around her as she
opened the door from his side. 'Sorry, but I couldn't
have been much quicker.'

Zac entered and she exited. He didn't bother to lock
the door, she noticed, but she did. She slid the lock
from inside her bedroom and glanced impatiently at it
as the sound of Zac's laughter reached her.

Cindy dressed quickly but carefully. She laddered the
first pair of tights she put on, discarded the second pair
because the shade wasn't right and was astonished to
find Zac sitting with a drink in his hand when she
emerged. And the glass was almost empty.

'I know women are renowned——' He broke off as
he took in the sight of her.

Cindy's stomach contracted just as it had when she'd
first set eyes on Zac. There were split seconds of silence,
appraisal, appreciation, just as there had been then.
She'd never seen him in a dark velvet evening jacket
before, or a dress shirt. He looked magnificent as he
stood up and held a hand out to her. Tall, broad,
immaculate and—yes, handsome was the right word.
Strikingly handsome.

'Well, this was certainly worth waiting for.' He spoke
quietly as he took her hand. Cindy turned towards a
chair, but Zac held her right where she stood, his glance
taking in the elegant black dress with its deep vee and
the provocative swell of her breasts.

The air between them was charged; the nearness of
him, the sight of him, the touch of his hand making
Cindy's heart pound so quickly she was sure he would
hear it.

She forced her eyes away from his, away from the
desire, the hunger so plainly and openly reflected there.
'Zac, please, I don't——'

'I do.' He said it very quietly as he imprisoned her in
his arms. His lips claimed hers with an electrifying

sensuality, tasting, exploring, the very intimacy of his kiss setting her body aflame with longing. She pulled away from him, caught in the battle between her body and her mind.

'Zac, please! *I don't want this!* If you want the truth, you frighten me. *This* frightens me——'

'*Truth*, Cindy? How can you tell me one thing when your body tells me something else? Wouldn't it be more honest to——' he caught hold of her hips and pulled her tightly against him. With one arm he held her there, impossibly, provokingly close, his free hand entwining itself in her hair as his mouth came down on hers, drugging her senses, turning her protests into lies. Slowly, subtly, the kiss changed as Cindy responded helplessly, then recklessly, everything in her straining to get closer to him.

Zac raised his head, but he did not release her. He held her against his body, his taut thighs pressing against her own, the hardness of his chest brushing against her breasts. He looked down at her, her lovely face flushed with desire, her lips parted by a small, anguished cry.

'You would deny this?' He released her, cupping her chin with his hand so she was forced to look at him. 'Still?' he demanded. 'Would you deny it now?'

Zac's eyes had darkened with a desire that matched her own, but they were not smiling. Nor was there a look of satisfaction in them.

Nor was there any warmth.

Anger flared through her at his audacity, his bluntness, his cold-blooded attitude. What right had he to assume, just *assume*, that she was there for the taking? But even as she thought this, she could feel his lips on her neck, his hands sliding from her waist to the curve of her hip. She felt the prickle of tears behind her eyes. Tears born of anger, frustration, self-loathing because she still couldn't fight him off. Damn it all, she didn't want to fight him off!'

With a man like Zac it would be all or nothing. And

to a man like him, it would be meaningless. If she didn't resist him she would end up as just another statistic in his love life—his *sex* life. He didn't care for her. He only wanted to possess her! She was a challenge to him—and he'd told her he never could resist a challenge.

She pulled away from him sharply, turning her back on him and closing her eyes against the tears that threatened to spill over. 'Zac, I can't deny the physical. It was there between us from the moment we met. I know it, you know it. This is what you once referred to when you mentioned your very first impression. Is that honest enough for you?' Her voice rose as she turned to meet his eyes. 'But with my mind I reject it! Do you understand? With my *mind* I reject the idea of having an affair with my boss! I reject the idea of spoiling our relationship when we've only just established it. I reject the idea of spoiling things as far as work's concerned. I reject above all the very thought of being physically intimate with a man I don't even care for!'

The telephone started ringing before she'd finished speaking. Zac didn't even look at it. He was looking at Cindy thoughtfully, strangely, and there was a muscle working in his jaw. Dear Lord, he didn't believe a word she'd said! How much truth there was in Cindy's last statement, she didn't really know. She knew only that words were her only defence against him. Words. 'I mean it, Zac. Every word of it . . . You'd better—you'd better answer the phone.'

For a long moment he didn't move. He just smiled. 'You'd better go and repair your lipstick. That'll be Alain.' He snatched up the phone as Cindy told him she needed a few minutes.

'Meet us in the bar, then,' he said quickly. 'Hello . . .?'

Cindy escaped into the bathroom and sat on the edge of the bath. She was suddenly dreading the evening ahead of her. How could she cope with an important business man, a total stranger, when she was being torn to pieces inside? And later, after dinner, what would happen then . . .?

She had been in no immediate danger just now, but there were two, possibly three, nights to get through before they returned to England.

Trembling, she struggled to regain her composure. She ran cold water over her wrists and hands and held them to her cheeks. She repaired her lipstick, combed her hair and dabbed beneath her eyes with a tissue, grateful that she'd at least managed to keep her tears in check.

Her reflection in the mirror was pleasing, that of a cool blonde who was calm and composed and had everything under control. It belied totally how she was feeling inside.

She walked into the bar looking confident, a tall, slender girl in an expensive black crêpe dress which showed off her figure to perfection. But she was unaware of the heads that turned to look at her. She saw only the sudden interest in the eyes of the man who was sitting with Zac, the way he got swiftly to his feet as she smiled at them on her approach.

Zac rose gracefully and lazily to his feet and pulled out a chair for Cindy as he made the introductions. 'Cindy, this is Alain Gérard. Alain, my secretary, Cindy Hetherington.'

It was difficult to guess the man's age. He could have been in his late fifties, he could have been in his middle sixties. He was about Cindy's height, with thick steely grey hair and dark eyebrows. He looked very distinguished, and Cindy acknowledged that he was still a good-looking man.

His appraisal of Cindy was quite open as he lifted her hand and pressed his lips to the back of it. *'Enchanté, mademoiselle, enchanté!'*

'Monsieur.' Cindy inclined her head politely, waiting for him to release her hand. He seemed reluctant to do so and when she sat, crossing one slender leg over another, Monsieur Gérard's eyes followed the movement.

'This is indeed a pleasure. Ah, indeed!' He bowed as he sat, and Cindy had to bite her cheeks to prevent her smile turning into a grin. He was typically French; in his greeting, his mannerisms, his charm. But his captivation with Cindy was perfectly genuine. 'Zac, if I had known this business was to be brightened by the presence of such a beautiful lady I would never have argued with you for a moment!'

Zac looked at Cindy, a sardonic smile playing around his mouth. 'Alain has a predilection for English ladies. You married one, isn't that right, Alain?'

The Frenchman shrugged as if he were not going to commit himself to an answer.

'What will you have to drink, Cindy?'

'Dry Martini.' She turned to Monsieur Gérard. 'So your wife is English? What part of the country is she from?'

'Dorset.'

'That's nice. And no doubt she is partly responsible for your command of English. May I congratulate you, Monsieur Gérard, on an extremely impressive accent— or should I say lack of one?'

'Alain, please!' He was delighted with her praise. 'Such a charming secretary you have, Zac. I envy you! Such warmth in an Englishwoman is rare, no?'

Cindy kept her eyes on Alain as Zac's answer came drily. To her ears, cuttingly. 'Yes. Very rare.'

As Zac had anticipated, the session in the bar was a long one. Alain was obviously a seasoned drinker and even more obviously in no hurry to get home to his wife. He never even mentioned business until they were drinking coffee after their meal.

By then Cindy had a slight headache. She hadn't drunk much, but she'd waited a long time for her dinner. There was also the tension between herself and Zac. She was no longer angry with him, she was simply aware of him. The tension was a sexual one, and she felt as if she were walking on the edge of a precipice.

'Ten o'clock,' Alain was saying. 'I and my Board will

see you at ten, but I can offer you no encouragement, Zac. I explained the situation on the telephone. You've missed the boat, as you English would say.'

'The Welsh say it, too.' Zac grinned. 'Well, we'll see, Alain. We'll see.'

Alain looked at Cindy, shrugging expansively, and she turned her mind on to the business in hand. She leaned forward slightly. 'Alain, I understand there are three other agencies pitching for this business . . .'

'Ach! My dear, everyone and his dog would like to handle this launch!'

'But of course!' Cindy waved a slender hand in the air, but it was towards the low neckline of her dress that Alain's eyes flitted before he looked at her directly. 'Any launch is exciting—and an entirely new range of Germaine products is doubly so. But you haven't mentioned when these other agencies will be presenting their speculative campaigns to you.'

'Next week. At the end of next week.'

The end of next week! It came as a shock to Cindy; she'd thought Bryant's might have three weeks or so in which to prepare a campaign. Surely Zac knew this? Surely he'd been told over the phone?

Of course he had! He was just more crazy than she thought. She didn't react with any surprise, she didn't even pause before asking her next question. 'I take it the gentlemen on your Board are aware, fully aware, of Zac's expertise in television advertising? I ask this because while I'm aware that you and Zac have known each other many years, your company does not in fact advertise their really expensive perfumes through the mass media. So I ask myself, do they know that Zac is the best in the business?'

Neither man smiled at her.

'I couldn't have put it better myself,' said Zac, in a matter-of-fact voice.

'Yes, yes. A fair question, Cindy.' Alain drained his coffee cup, watching her approvingly. 'Believe me, if this were my decision alone, I would give the business to any agency headed by Zac. I need no persuasion. There is one member of the Board who thinks likewise. He ...' Alain broke off, searching for a word, '... lamented that we hadn't known of Zac's return to advertising earlier. However, it isn't this man's decision, either. You understand, the Board have to be unanimous on this, something so important. Alas, we are two against four others who will not be persuaded, for purely practical reasons. The brief was given to your competitors over eight weeks ago. As I say, Bryant's are simply too late.'

At that, Zac smiled and suggested they adjourn to the lounge for more coffee and brandy. When they got up from the table he kept the conversation well away from business. Really, there was no more to be said.

'Cindy, I was wondering if you'd like to go on somewhere else?' The question came from Alain as soon as they'd settled in the lounge. 'In Paris, the night is young no matter what the hour! Perhaps you would like to see a show—perhaps a little dancing? What do you think? And you, Zac?'

Cindy's heart plummeted. She was fit to drop, her headache had worsened. Actually, the entire evening had been quite a strain. She glanced quickly at her boss and saw that his face was impassive. Almost. She could read those eyes well enough to know without doubt that he was laughing inwardly. She knew also what he was going to say. Damn him! He was about to say that here was her perfect opportunity to see some night life—which was just what she'd asked for in the taxi that afternoon.

But she was quite, quite wrong. 'Not tonight, Alain,' Zac said firmly. 'Cindy has been working extremely hard of late and it really would be unfair of me to keep her out of bed tonight. I'm sure she's tired.'

The ambiguity, of course, went over Alain's head. Determined not even to look at Zac, Cindy turned to the older man. 'You know, I'd have loved to, Alain. But to be honest I have a slight headache and I am rather tired, what with the journey and all. But thank you anyway.'

Alain clapped his hands together in mock despair. 'Maybe some other time, Cindy? Who knows, when I'm next in England maybe you will offer to show me some of the night life in London?'

It was a gentlemanly acceptance of a lady's decision, but neither Zac nor Cindy made any mistake as to what was going through Alain's mind. 'Who knows?' she said lightly. 'As you say, Alain.'

Cindy excused herself after half an hour or so, pleading a worsening headache due to her tiredness. Actually, she'd never felt more alert in her life, though she honestly did have a headache.

Zac came to the suite almost an hour later. The doors were locked, of course, and Cindy's light was off, but she waited nonetheless for him to come to her room, or to hear some sort of taunt about the lack of originality in the way she'd made her escape from him.

But she needn't have worried. Zac came nowhere near her bedroom door. Nor did he make any comment through the bathroom door. Yet he was, she just knew, aware that she was awake.

'. . . Whatever decision is reached today, gentlemen, you are going to benefit from this meeting. You're planning to spend three quarters of a million pounds sterling on advertising to get your new range off the ground. The choice as to which agency will handle that for you is a major decision. Monsieur Gérard has made it clear to me that three agencies are well on their way in preparing speculative campaigns for you.' Zac shrugged slightly, looking from one face to the next. 'And I am here, as Chairman and Managing Director of Bryant's of London—rather late in the day—to give you the benefit of my experience.'

There was a nod here, a rather uninterested twist of the lips there, a wry smile from Germaine's Sales Director and a very light strumming of fingers on the

Board room table. Cindy looked around the room without moving her head, feeling a nervous anxiety which Zac Stone had long since become incapable of feeling. Including Alain, he was addressing four members of the Board, plus the Export Sales Manager and the Advertising Manager of Germaine's. They were a mixed bunch, as were their individual reactions as Zac continued to speak.

But they were listening.

Zac had been talking for five minutes, uninterrupted. After the first couple of minutes it had become obvious that the Financial Director was having difficulty in keeping up with a foreign language, at which point Cindy's nervousness had increased as she waited for Zac's signal that she should interpret for him.

But Zac had given her barely more than a glance since they'd entered the room and he was talking, now, in fluent French with a strong Parisian accent . . . far better than she could speak the language. And she spoke it well.

Would she ever really get to know about Zac? All about Zac? Would he continue forever to surprise her, to fascinate her? She glanced at him, sharp and immaculate in an expensive lightweight suit and a white shirt, his keen eyes no doubt monitoring every reaction, every facial expression of the individuals around him.

She wished that he didn't have this . . . this hold over her. She felt that she was not fully in control of herself, and that was something Cindy disliked. Still she was unable to define what it was about Zac that held her so, quite what it was she felt for him. Whatever it was, it was outside her experience. It was certainly more than physical attraction. Unlike him, their relationship meant more to her than that.

There had been that fleeting moment when she'd thought she might be falling in love with him. But how was she to recognise it, if that were the case? It had never happened to her before. She'd dismissed the idea, and she dismissed it again now. She hadn't met a man yet with whom she'd fallen in love. And she'd met her fair share of them.

'. . . The importance of market research. I'm talking about finding out who your customers are going to be, what they want, what they *think* they want, from a product such as yours. What motivates women to buy toiletries and perfume?'

There followed a veritable hubbub of conversation. Zac's question was met with a dozen answers. The Marketing Director scribbled something on a sheet of paper in front of him, and Alain Gérard said nothing.

Zac turned his hands palms upwards. 'Of course, gentlemen, of course. Those are the obvious answers. On the face of things, I would agree with you. But would you be more specific? What is the result of the research these agencies have undertaken for you?' Zac's eyes went directly to those of the Advertising Manager and it was obvious he was put out by the question.

'Mr Stone,' the Financial Director spoke up, 'we're making only a nominal contribution towards the expenses for the work your competitors are undertaking for us. Their incentive to spend their own money is obvious. But we haven't asked them to risk their money on intensive market research.'

'Risk?' Zac parroted. 'You're talking about spending peanuts when you're offering a budget of three quarters of a million, when the success or failure of your product is at stake? Are you telling me my competitors haven't *insisted* on doing their homework?'

'Well, Cooksons are doing a certain amount of research on the——' the Ad Manager started to defend himself.

'Packaging.' Zac finished for him. 'Yes, I'm aware of Cooksons' methods, their way of thinking. They're good, gentlemen, but by no means good enough.'

Zac went into full swing; he'd seen his competitors' weaknesses and exploited them to the fullest. He fired a dozen questions as to the anticipated sales of the entire range, which was set out in the centre of the table.

In his role as Chairman, Alain did little other than maintain a quiet order about things as the meeting hotted up. The Advertising Manager had gone rather quiet, but it was he who finally spoke up and suggested to the other men that Bryant's be given the opportunity of preparing a speculative campaign. This was instantly seconded by the Financial Director.

Cindy hid her glee behind an impassive face, but her boss's next words shocked her as much as they shocked the others.

'You misunderstand me, gentlemen. I'm *not willing* to prepare a speculative campaign for you.'

There followed total silence, then ten minutes during which Zac explained to them exactly what his position was, what his methods were. He asked questions of the various men present, pertinent to their particular role, and got the fullest co-operation from everyone except the Marketing Director. The Marketing Director refused to reveal certain information about the company's sales procedures, arguing that this was strictly confidential and that it would be given only to the agency who was finally chosen to do their advertising.

Zac looked at his watch, and Cindy surreptitiously glanced at hers. It was almost noon, but they weren't in any hurry . . .

'To summarise,' Zac got to his feet, and all eyes were on him, 'I am not willing to prepare a campaign based on guesswork. Let my competitors come up with a series of pretty pictures; they do not deserve your business.' He looked at the Ad Manager, 'As I'm sure you will agree, *Monsieur*. Either you decide to give me the business or you don't. I appreciate that you'll have to decide quickly, and we'll leave you now to do just that. Monsieur Gérard knows where I can be contacted. I'll be in Paris until Friday noon. If your answer is yes, you must be prepared to give me all your secrets.' He turned, then, to the Marketing Director. 'I want to know every last detail of how your sales network functions. Be assured of one thing: my creative team, my artists, will not pick up a pen until Bryant's know exactly what type of woman we are aiming at with these products—and for what reason she is likely to buy them, until we have a clear idea of anticipated sales in the North of England compared to the Midlands or the South. Television advertising is an expensive business, as you're well aware. We don't want to waste money on air time in one region when it would be better to cover the area with a different approach. And so on and so on.

'Thank you for your time, gentlemen. It was a pleasure meeting you. Now if you'll excuse us, Miss Hetherington and I have other business in Paris this afternoon.'

CHAPTER NINE

'WHAT other business?' Cindy asked the question the moment they stepped out into the street. The sun was shining from a perfectly blue sky and she took the arm Zac extended to her as they strolled along in the shade of the buildings.

'Lunch, of course,' he grinned at her.

Cindy giggled, but her mind was still whirling from the meeting that had just taken place. Zac had done a superb job, but she was not optimistic about Bryant's being given the business. She told him this, and she queried the wisdom of his tactics in refusing to compete with the other agencies.

'That wasn't a tactic, Cindy.' He turned left and then cut down an alleyway of cobblestones, knowing, it seemed, exactly where they were going. 'I don't prepare campaigns for people who aren't my clients. I don't need to these days. Either they entrust their business, their money, into my hands or they don't. Do you like seafood?'

'I love it.' She looked at him curiously. 'So what do we do now?'

'We wait for the telephone to ring. In the meantime, relax and enjoy yourself. It's in the bag.'

He seemed so confident that his mission had been successful. Cindy sucked in her breath, appalled. 'Zac! That really is tempting fate. I thought you were superstitious about counting your chickens ... No, I mean *talking* about it?'

'I am. But not when it's a dead cert. That Ad Manager should be fired.'

'But he was on your side!'

Zac laughed shortly. 'Only because I made him aware of his incompetence. He'll save his neck from the chopping block if he votes to give me the business, and he knows it. He knows the launch will be a success if I handle it. Now, that's enough, Cindy. No more shop talk. Except . . .' He smiled at her, his eyes twinkling with amusement. 'Except to say you did well last night. I meant to tell you over breakfast.'

Cindy pursed her lips and shrugged it off. 'Well, I was on duty, after all. Someone had to blow your trumpet for you. It wasn't for you to do it—though you're perfectly capable!'

He squeezed her arm. 'I wasn't referring to the plug you gave me. I was referring to the diplomatic way you handled Alain's attentions—the old goat. He fancies you like mad!'

'Don't be so unkind! He's not an old goat. He's a good-looking man.'

'Do you know how old he is?' Zac admonished.

She looked at him mischievously. 'I've always preferred older men.'

'I'm glad to hear it.' His blue eyes moved over her face and lingered fleetingly on the gentle curve of her lips. She was sorry she'd spoken.

'Cindy, Alain has always been a ladies' man. He's a well-practised charmer. When he comes to London, I warn you, don't give him the slightest encouragement. For heaven's sake, he's forty years older than you! He's old enough to be your father—your grandfather!'

'Ah!' she smiled, teasing him, unwilling to let him have the last word. 'But he's not my grandfather.'

They walked at a leisurely pace through a network of streets and alleys in a romantic city that was drenched in sunshine, throbbing with activity, fascinating in its mysteries. Lunch, for Cindy, was a new experience; they took a river cruise on the Seine and ate fresh seafood and crispy salad, washed down with superb French wine. They were killing time—but what a lovely way to do it! And Zac was the perfect companion, knowledgeable, amusing, charming.

In the late afternoon they took a taxi to Notre Dame

and browsed the bookstalls and art displays on the embankment of the Seine, watching the artists at work. It was turned seven when they got back to the George V and ordered a pot of coffee to be sent to their suite.

Cindy sank wearily but contentedly into an armchair in the sitting room and kicked off her shoes. 'What will we do this evening, Zac? I don't think I have the energy for more sightseeing. Oh, but I enjoyed this afternoon! Thank you.'

He smiled at her enthusiasm, at her lovely, vivacious face. 'You don't need to walk anywhere, except into a taxi which will be waiting at the door. I'm taking you to Le Moulin Rouge. How does that grab you?'

'Oh!' Cindy squealed with delight. 'It grabs me!' She was laughing at the expression he'd used, at the way he was laughing at her laughter, when the telephone rang.

Her laughter died in her throat as she looked from the telephone to her boss. Her fingers went to the thin, gold chain at her neck and fiddled with it nervously.

It was Alain.

Cindy held her breath as Zac spoke to him. If they landed this business, it would be the making of Bryant's. She wanted so much for that to happen, for Zac, for everyone concerned. But her boss's face was unsmiling, his words sparse.

'I see . . .' He glanced at Cindy, but he wasn't really seeing her. He was looking through her, beyond her, his mind concentrated only on what he was hearing. '. . . And when did they reach their decision? Ten minutes ago, eh?'

Cindy's heart sank like a stone as Zac let out a long, slow breath. He leaned back in his chair and that giveaway muscle was moving in his jaw. Whether he was angry or just disappointed, she couldn't tell.

'. . . You had quite a discussion, by the sound of it. Okay, Alain, thank you for letting me know at once . . . Of course . . . yes, do that.'

Zac put down the phone. He hooked one long, powerful leg over an arm of his chair and let his eyes drift toward the window, his fingers strumming against his thigh.

'Zac, I'm so sorry . . .'

He didn't hear her.

Cindy felt suddenly embarrassed; she didn't know what else to say to him. She also felt crushed with disappointment.

More than a minute passed before he turned to look at her. 'I'm sorry, Cindy? What was that?'

'I—I said I'm sorry. About Germaine's. It—there was nothing else you could have done this morning. You said it all. I—it was in the lap of the gods.'

Zac nodded. 'And the gods were kind. We've got the account, Cindy.' Very quietly, he added, 'It's ours, all ours. Without any conditions or reservations. Cooksons and the other people will be informed in the morning.'

Cindy's mouth opened in astonishment. She couldn't believe her ears. She wanted to wave her arms about, to jump up and down or something. But of course that wasn't her style. And quite apart from that, Zac Stone didn't seem in the least happy with the news. He didn't seem unhappy, either. He was just—just miles away in his thoughts.

'Zac, what is it? Why are you looking like that? What are you thinking?'

'Mm?' He looked through her again. 'Cindy, why don't you go and rest for a while? I——' He smiled then, but it was as if he were making an effort to do so. 'I have some thinking to do. Have a sleep, then put on something spectacular and we'll paint the town red. We don't have to be at Germaine's until eleven tomorrow. Okay?'

'Okay.' She smiled brightly. He wanted to be left alone. The evening he was planning was for her sake, she knew. And he wasn't going to tell her what was going through his mind.

Cindy took a leisurely bath. She felt disturbed, unhappy because Zac's reaction to the news wasn't what it should be. But she was probably worrying needlessly. No doubt his mind had simply zoomed ahead. He'd probably started plotting and planning for Germaine's as soon as he received the good news!

At a little before ten she padded into the bathroom and put on her make-up. Her robe was still in the bedroom and she was brushing her hair when Zac suddenly walked in on her.

'Oh. Sorry, but the door wasn't——'

The door wasn't locked. Sleepy from her nap, she'd forgotten to lock either of them. It was entirely her own fault.

Cindy slowly put down her hairbrush as she turned to face him. He was motionless, tall and broad and frighteningly attractive as he stood in the doorway to his bedroom. He was half-naked, barefoot, covered only by a white bathtowel which was tucked in at the waist.

And Cindy's body wasn't covered by anything.

She knew, the instant her eyes met with his, that it was too late. Too late for protests, too late for words. They were about to become lovers and there wasn't a thing in the world she could do about it.

She spoke his name quietly. Just once.

Neither of them moved.

Every nerve in Cindy's body sprang to life with a yearning she would never have believed herself capable of feeling. As Zac's eyes slowly roamed the length of her naked body, her pulses leapt as they did every time he'd touched her.

His look, his absorption with her now, was in itself a caress. She, too, was like someone mesmerised as she drank in the sight of him, the slow rise and fall of a magnificent chest darkened with hair; his skin, so tanned that it seemed polished, perfect.

Zac's face was sombre, his blue eyes darkening perceptively as he started to speak. But no words came. His lips closed and his mouth was unsmiling as he opened his arms to Cindy as she walked into his embrace.

He didn't kiss her. He just looked at her and let his hands travel very, very lightly over her face, her throat, her shoulders, her breasts. His hands trembled slightly as they moved, infinitely slowly, over every curve and contour of her body. She saw his eyes close, as though he would store indelibly in his mind every detail of her.

'Beautiful . . .' Zac's voice had roughened, deepened so that it was barely recognisable. 'You are incredibly, perfectly beautiful.'

Cindy closed the distance between their bodies, pressing tightly against the length of him. Her lips went to the base of his throat as her arms closed around the broad expanse of his back. Her blood was on fire, pounding through her veins. She could hardly breathe, her heart was racing so fast.

Gently, he loosened her hold on him, his breathing accelerating slightly as he spoke to her. 'Easy, my darling. We have all the time in the world. All the time . . .'

She was desperate for his kiss, her entire body trembling, screaming for his touch, and at the instant when she thought she could no longer stand, Zac lifted her into his arms in one easy, effortless movement and carried her into his room.

There was a moment, just one fleeting moment, when a voice in the farthest recesses of Cindy's mind tried to make itself heard. It was a voice which sounded so much like her own, barely audible but plaintive. 'Tomorrow, I'll regret this . . . I'll hate myself . . . in the morning . . .'

Then Zac's mouth closed over hers and the voice was obliterated. His lips trailed over her face, her eyes, her pulsating temples, as he lowered her on to his bed. 'Darling Cindy, no.' His breath was a warm breeze against her hair. 'I know exactly how you're going to feel in the morning . . .' He laughed softly as he lay beside her, naked now, kissing her, caressing, stroking.

Cindy moaned under his touch, his expert exploration of her was a torch to the fire that had been kindling from the first time they met. She would never have dreamt it possible for a man to understand a woman's body, a woman's needs, the way Zac did. It seemed that there was a merging of minds, of spirits, as they caressed each other—discovering, delighting, savouring. With every passing moment, every touch, Cindy sank deeper and deeper into a state which was at once an oblivion and an awakening.

And Zac was still very much in control, of himself, of her, as he brought her slowly, deliberately, deliciously, to an all-consuming, devastating frenzy of longing. She cried out to him, unable any longer to bear the torture that was the ache inside her. Unable to wait for the moment when he would take her.

'Zac . . . Oh, please! Zac!' She stilled his hands, trembling uncontrollably as she arched towards him. Zac went on kissing her, his breathing ragged as his lips closed over the sensitive tips of her breasts, taunting, nibbling, gently sucking until she gasped from the exquisite torment of it.

Zac's muscles felt rigid under the smoothness of his skin as Cindy locked her arms around him, pulling him close until his mouth closed over hers in a deep and deliciously erotic exchange.

For the merest instant, Cindy's mind blotted out as Zac groaned against her lips. He drew her even closer and held her in the crook of one arm as his fingers moved towards that most intimate part of her. His lips moved lightly over her mouth in a taunting series of kisses, and within seconds Cindy was crying out as wave after wave of pure physical ecstasy shook her body.

She lay, fighting for breath, momentarily passive in Zac's arms as he smiled into her eyes and covered her face with kisses. She was unable to take her eyes from his, was unable to believe the intensity of what she had just experienced. Zac was kissing the outermost corners of her eyes, her forehead, her cheeks, as if he would reward her for her responsiveness, her very femininity.

She gazed at him with disbelieving eyes as her passion flared again, instantly, as he continued to caress her.

'Cindy . . .' he laid her against the pillows, his voice, his movement telling her there was no turning back now. A wave of anxiety crept unbidden into Cindy's mind. She stiffened slightly as she looked at Zac's powerful body, wanting him as she had never wanted any other man . . . As she had never known any other man.

She reached for him a little fearfully, the trembling of her hands, the tremor in her voice, beyond her control. 'Zac, please . . . Will you . . . I've never—I mean, I've never . . .'

For as long as she lived, she would never, ever, forget the look in Zac's eyes at that moment in time.

'God in heaven . . .' he looked at her in disbelief, his voice less than a whisper. 'I don't believe this. I don't— Cindy, *what are you telling me?*'

'I——' Cindy's voice was locked in her throat. She couldn't say it. Her eyes closed involuntarily because her mind refused to cope with what was happening. She couldn't bear the way Zac was looking at her. She had seen the muscles of his arms go rigid, his entire body stiffen as he moved, just a few inches, away from her.

'Zac, please, it's all right. It's all right——' Blindly she reached for him, but as her hands touched his chest, she felt Zac's fingers close around her wrists.

'Cindy——' he moved away from her completely, his breathing laboured as he fought for control. 'Cindy, you don't . . . oh, *God!*' She opened her eyes as he swore under his breath, his fingers raking the hair from his forehead. 'Did I get it wrong,' he muttered. 'Oh, boy, did I get it wrong this time! Why the hell didn't you——'

He stopped short as he saw the tears on her face. 'Cindy, I can't believe this. I had no idea. Why the hell didn't you tell me before now? How could you take such a——'

Cindy was crying silently but uncontrollably. She

turned over and buried her face in the pillow, wishing she could die. She felt humiliated. Not by Zac, for he was controlling his anger far more than she deserved. She felt ashamed of herself. She'd known what he was going to say to her, and he was right.

'Stop that!' She felt his hand brush lightly over her hair, but she couldn't look at him. 'Stop it now, Cindy. It's . . .' She heard him sigh from the depths of his being, felt the bed give as he stood up. 'It's all right. Darling, I—I'm going down to the bar. Come and join me when you feel ready. I—we'll eat in the hotel restaurant.'

Several minutes passed before he left the room. There was the sound of drawers opening and closing as he got dressed and then, mercifully, she was alone. Her tears stopped when he'd gone and she turned over and stared blindly at the ceiling. Never in her life had she felt so wretched, so desperately unhappy. She had to face it: she was deeply in love with Zac—and it was utterly, utterly hopeless. Pointless. A man such as he would never want a permanent relationship with a woman, *one* woman. He'd never settle down if he lived to be a hundred. He hadn't even been able to settle into retirement. He'd missed the challenge of his work. Work made him tick. It was the only thing that really brought him to life.

And there had been, obviously, many women in his life. There would be more. One affair after the next. As there had been in the past. When he took time off from work, that was. When he felt the need.

Cindy got to her feet, only to sink wearily back on to the bed. She sat, crouched forward, her arms wrapped tightly around her ribs as if it would ease the pain inside her. What was the point of loving someone like Zac? Someone so very different from herself? There was no sense in it; there was no sense in the fact that it had happened in the first place. She couldn't just decide to fall out of love with him. Love wasn't something that could be turned on and off, like a tap. Oh, but why, *why*, of all the men in the world did it have to be him?

After a while, Cindy got up and went to her own room. She pulled on her robe, feeling suddenly very cold. As much as she disliked strong drinks she needed one now if she'd ever needed one.

She was sipping her way through a neat whisky when the phone rang.

'Cindy, how long do I have to wait before you put in an appearance?'

'I'm not coming down, Zac.'

'I want to talk to you,' he said tiredly. 'Come down and eat with me.'

'No.' She put the phone down. She would have to face Zac sooner or later, but she certainly couldn't face him in a restaurant full of people.

More than an hour passed before he came back to the suite. He found her sitting in her room near the open window.

'I've brought you some sandwiches.' He plonked a plate on to the table at her side.

'Have you eaten?'

'Of course I've eaten,' he snapped. 'I couldn't wait for ever.'

She looked up at him then, her eyes narrowing. 'Are you drunk?'

'Nowhere near.' He sighed, lowering himself into the chair opposite hers. 'Just slightly . . . anaesthetised.'

Cindy flushed with embarrassment. 'I—I'm sorry, Zac. I—feel very badly about that.'

'Don't worry about it.' He laughed humourlessly. 'I can always take a cold bath.'

She flinched inwardly at his bluntness; she was only too aware of what she'd done to him and she wasn't exactly proud of it.

He ran a hand tiredly through his hair. 'I take it you're not on the pill? I mean, for some other reason, perhaps?'

'Zac, *must* you?' Cindy hardly knew where to look. 'I really don't——'

'Answer me, dammit!'

'No,' she said dully, 'I'm not.'

He lost his temper then—finally. He got up and stalked about the room as Cindy closed her eyes against his all too evident anger. 'I thought as much! What the devil were you thinking about? How could you take a risk like that? After all I've told you about my past. And you were so quick to remind me that once is all it takes! How could you be so bloody irresponsible? Well, you can count yourself lucky that I never knowingly take a risk. You can count yourself lucky I've got a neurotic streak about this sort of thing. We have my scheming bitch of an ex-wife to thank for that! I don't walk twice into the same trap!'

'Trap? Trap!' She glared at him, her embarrassment forgotten. She was fighting to keep her own anger in check now. 'I understand how you feel—obviously. But I'd had no intention of making love with you—ever! Kindly remember that!' The last thing she wanted to do then was to cry. But she couldn't help it. She was angry; she was loving Zac and hating him at the same time. She was confused and she felt incredibly sad that something which had been so beautiful and spontaneous should be dissected like this. 'Get out of here, will you? Just get out and leave me alone——' She choked on a sob, her hands flying up to cover her face.

Zac apologised instantly. 'I'm sorry.' She felt his hands on her shoulders, but she couldn't look at him. 'Cindy, I'm sorry. Really. Here——' he handed her his hanky. 'Don't cry—please. I can't stand it.' She heard him let out a long, ragged breath. 'Cindy, it isn't really you I'm angry with. It's me. You see, I—I never dreamt you were . . . I'm mad as hell because I had it all wrong! I thought I knew you, but I didn't. I thought you were just enjoying the fun of the chase. Dear God—a virgin, yet!'

He went to the fridge and took out two miniatures of Scotch. 'Since when do you drink whisky? Never mind. Here, have another!'

If he was trying to get her to smile, he failed. 'I've never encouraged you,' she said accusingly. 'Please remember that.'

Zac looked heavenward, the air whistling past his teeth. 'Your very existence is encouragement in itself.' He sat down, shaking his head. He was quiet for a long time.

Cindy said nothing. She sipped at her drink and resigned herself to his presence. He wouldn't leave her alone until he was good and ready. He'd made a mistake in his assessment of this particular woman. Maybe his professional pride was injured?

'We have to talk,' he said at length. 'You see, the more I get to know about you, the less I know you. It's—you have an amazing ability to give people entirely the wrong impression. Do you know that? At first I thought you were a stuck-up, haughty little snob. Then I discovered your sense of humour, your sensitivity, your abilities as far as work's concerned, your sophistication . . . *apparent* sophistication. Now I find out that beneath your veneers you're just an old-fashioned girl! You never cease to surprise me, Cindy.'

'If you're trying to put me down,' she said coldly, 'it won't work. Not this time. I'm not an old-fashioned girl, I just don't——'

'Wait a minute, wait a minute!' Zac held up a hand. 'I'm not trying to put you down—I'm trying to understand you. I want to talk to you. Give me a chance. I want you to see how things have looked from my point of view. All right?'

'All right,' she shrugged carelessly.

'Now, you told me that during your first couple of years in London you had a wild time. You said you did all the things you'd wanted to do, you had fun, you went out with lots of men——'

'I did. But I wasn't involved with any one of them. It didn't include——'

'Let me finish! From my point of view, Cindy, remember? I've found you to be—responsive, to say the least. I had every intention of taking you to bed . . . last week . . . next week . . . whenever the time was right.'

He laughed, making no secret of his inability to understand her. 'And now this! I'd like to know how you've got away with it.'

'I don't know what you mean,' she said dully. It had never been a question of Cindy 'getting away with' anything. But she could hardly tell Zac that he was the first man who'd ever really turned her on. Any more than she could tell him she was in love with him.

He looked at her in exasperation. 'There must have been someone, some time . . . What about the man who sent you those roses? What happened there?'

'James?'

'Whoever. How long had you been seeing him? Why did it finish?'

'He lied to me. He lied when he didn't need to.'

'How long?'

'I'd been seeing him for about four months.' Cindy shrugged. She didn't really see the point in this, but she was perfectly willing to tell Zac about James. 'I really liked him. We had a—a sort of intellectual relationship, I suppose.'

'A *what*?' Zac turned and looked at her as if she were unreal. 'What was wrong with him? How could a man have an intellectual relationship with you? Didn't he try to get you into bed?'

'Yes—in the beginning. And when I made it clear I wasn't interested, he accepted it. We were friends. He was a lecturer at the technical college—I used to go to evening classes there. He lectured in philosophy and we had some really interesting discussions.'

'I've heard everything now,' Zac said drily. 'So what happened?'

'He was seeing someone else at the same time. Sleeping with someone. No, don't look at me like that. Because I didn't care. That's the irony of it—I didn't care about that. I'm not some sort of prude, Zac. But James and I were supposed to have an honest relationship. We were free to do as we wished. It would have made no difference to me if he'd been seeing six other women. But he lied to me, and he didn't need to. That's what upset me. You see, I'd trusted him, and I don't trust easily. Any more than I can . . . give of myself easily.

'One day, I got a phone call from an hysterical female telling me to leave James alone! Can you imagine how I felt? I tried telling her it was strictly platonic between James and me, and I won't repeat what she said to that. Then she told me she'd been seeing James for almost a year. She was in love with him, she said, and she was sick of his unfaithfulness.'

Zac was leaning against the windowsill, his hands shoved into the pockets of his slacks. He was listening carefully, but he said nothing.

'I confronted James with it, and he apologised over and over again. He said he wanted to go on seeing me. He even went as far as saying he was in love with me. Ha! He said it was just sex with the other girl. It was the same old story, Zac—just sex. Anyway——' She waved a dismissive arm. 'That was the end of James. As far as I'm concerned he was a liar and a hypocrite. Within the context of our relationship, he was unfaithful to me, too. Fortunately, unlike this other girl, I was not in love with him.'

Zac shook his head slowly. 'You've got a thing about unfaithfulness, Cindy. The frequency with which you use the word . . . it probably started with your father, that incident you told me about, when you were thirteen. Your father was unfaithful to you then—and you've been on your guard ever since, as far as men are concerned. You don't trust, you don't give, you make no allowances for human nature. And you don't forgive, either.'

'Spare me,' she snapped. 'Spare me the armchair psychology. I've told you, my father was unfaithful to *my mother*. And if you think I'm an old-fashioned girl for finding that distasteful, then go ahead!'

'And I've told you,' he said quietly, 'your father was unfaithful to your image of him. So was James.'

'For heaven's sake!' Cindy was getting more irritated by the minute. 'Just leave me alone, will you? We're fundamentally different, you and I. Our attitudes are different. Let's leave it at that, shall we? I am as I am, and that's all there is to it. And if you find my . . . my past . . . amusing in some way, that's entirely up to you!'

'Oh, I'm not amused,' he said quietly. 'Not in the least. I don't have an aversion to virgins, you know. But it's been a long time since I found myself in bed with one, and as far as you're concerned . . . Well, let's say I had a rude awakening.'

Cindy gave him an oblique look, still uncertain whether he was laughing at her, and wondering what this conversation was leading to.

Zac lowered himself into a chair and stuck his feet on the windowsill, watching her all the time he spoke, unaware of the pain his words were causing her. 'You'll never find him, you know—this man you're looking for. This paragon—your ideal man who can give you a guarantee never to let you down. This man you've been saving yourself for.'

Cindy wanted to laugh and cry at the same time. 'You're not the first person to tell me I expect too much of people, Zac. But it's ludicrous to say I've been saving myself for someone! Because it sure as hell wasn't you! Yet I was willing to spend tonight in your bed—regardless.'

'Ah! But you'd have hated yourself in the morning. I didn't believe it when you told me, but I believe it now. I never had your acquiescence, Cindy. You wanted me with your body but not with your mind. You'd told me that, too, more than once.'

Cindy picked up her drink and swallowed it in one go. She didn't know how to answer that one. She was so afraid of giving her feelings away. If he suspected how she really felt about him, it would certainly give him cause for amusement. 'Zac, if you're trying to tie me up in knots, you're succeeding. What do you want of me?' She threw up her hands in exasperation. 'Where is this leading?'

'I'm trying to solve your problem.'

'I don't have a problem.'

'Don't you?' he smiled sardonically. 'You're mine for the taking, Cindy—any time, anywhere. I know it, and you know it. You have no more shocks in store for me. I've discovered, finally, the real Cindy Hetherington.'

With that, he got to his feet. Cindy couldn't move a muscle. She was trembling, at a loss to understand him.

Zac put a hand under her chin, tilting her face up to his as he looked steadily into her eyes. 'I'll leave you now, Cindy. I've got some thinking to do. A little . . . reassessment.'

She brazened it out, meeting his gaze squarely. 'Indeed? You see, Zac, you didn't know me at all, did you?'

He kissed her lightly on the mouth. 'I wasn't referring to you, actually. I had something quite different on my mind before I walked into that bathroom tonight. But that's strictly my problem. As for yourself, may I suggest that you spend the next hour or so coming to terms with your own problem? How are you going to reconcile youself to having an affair with a man you don't even care for? I quote yesterday's words, Cindy.' He pulled her to her feet roughly, and even as she hated him for taunting her, his nearness was affecting her more than ever before.

She snatched her hands from his grasp. 'You're a ruthless, cold-blooded bastard——'

'And you want me. What an interesting situation this is!' He walked towards the door, smiling as he turned. 'We have to be at Germaine's at eleven tomorrow. I'll have breakfast brought to the sitting room at nine. You'll be working hard tomorrow. We have to record everything there is to know about that company and their products. So don't battle with yourself for too long. Get some sleep. You've learned something tonight, after all—you're just as susceptible to the power of sex as anyone else is. Goodnight, my beauty.'

CHAPTER TEN

THE days that followed were probably the strangest days of Cindy's life. She was in anguish, an agony of indecision.

In the office things were relatively slack. The Simpson campaign had been given the go-ahead and there was nothing Bryant's could do on the Germaine account until the results of the market research were to hand. It would be the beginning of September before things started to get hectic on Germaine's behalf.

Cindy had time to think. And rethink. Her evenings were free, and she went for a drive or a walk on every one of them. Zac let her leave the office at five each evening, though he stayed on himself, talking to Greg Halliday about Germaine's.

Over the weekend that followed she saw nothing of Zac. No doubt he was still hunting for a house in the country in which he would make his escape from the city on future weekends. When work permitted.

Cindy was functioning normally as far as work was concerned. Nobody could have suspected the inner turmoil she was going through. After dinner on the Sunday evening she sat down with a cup of coffee and tried to reach a positive decision.

She should leave Bryant's. If she were to hang on to her sanity, she should leave. But she couldn't. It had nothing to do with pride and nothing to do with interest in her work. In fact, she could no longer claim that. She was not, after all, so dedicated that she could work at a breakneck pace for the sake of work. Unlike Zac, she no longer found that the challenge was enough. Unlike Zac, she had found what was missing in her life. And that was something totally unattainable—Zac Stone, the man she had not been looking for. The man she had not been saving herself for.

James had once told her that she didn't know herself, and she'd denied it vehemently. But she didn't know herself now. It seemed that her life, her future, was crumbling around her. Since meeting Zac an insidious change had been taking place within her.

It was strange, really. In Paris, Zac had told her that the more he knew about her, the less he knew her. She felt exactly the same about him. She knew him better than she had before, yet she understood him less than ever.

But she loved him.

Whatever he was or was not—and he certainly was not the paragon he'd accused her of wanting—she loved him.

Nobody had told her what it was like to be in love. Nobody had told her it could be so painful. Nobody had told her how love could make a person behave illogically. She couldn't leave Bryant's, because she couldn't leave Zac.

There was neither rhyme nor reason in it, but there it was.

Nor could she enter into an affair with him. It would be the destruction of her. It would run its course, as all his previous affairs had, and leave Cindy—where? What? Empty. Desolate. As things stood, she could cope. But if Zac were to become her lover . . . well, the glory of that would be overshadowed by the inevitability of its outcome.

On the other hand, thinking in terms of inevitability, surely she was swimming against the tide? Oh, Zac hadn't made a move in that direction. But he would. He was playing cat and mouse with her. Maybe he was waiting, right now, for her to knock on his door and walk into his arms. Maybe he'd knock on her door first.

For more than a week, since the unforgettable evening in Paris, nothing had been said on a personal level. They had worked with one another, snapped at

one another, laughed together. And beyond all that, it
was still there. A burning desire, unsatisfied. With all its
inherent complications, promises and mysteries. Beyond
the most casual word, the most casual touch, it was
there, crackling in the air. Just as if it had a presence all
of its own.

Like Pandora's box.

It was on the Monday morning, ten days after they
had left Paris, that Cindy finally made a decision. She
walked into Zac's office with a well-rehearsed speech
about why she was handing her notice in.

As soon as she got through the door Zac looked up
from the chart he was working on and shoved a piece of
paper in Cindy's direction. 'I've just had Miss Druce in
here.' He said it without preamble. 'She's handed her
notice in—finally.'

'I—You were expecting it?'

He shrugged. 'Of course I was expecting it. She's
complained twice about the girls in the typing pool. You
saw the state she was in the last time she came in here.'

'Yes.' Cindy remembered only too clearly. 'But she
wouldn't tell me what was wrong. In what way was she
complaining? What about the girls in the typing pool?'

'It's their natural—youthful effervescence,' he
grinned. 'Miss Druce can't cope with it. Her ears and
her sensibilities are being offended daily.' He looked
heavenward. 'God bless her cotton socks.'

Cindy shoved a stack of files out of the way and sat
down. 'Zac, you knew she wouldn't last, didn't you?
But you had nowhere else to place her except the typing
pool, did you?'

'Nope.' He picked up his pen and went back to his
chart.

'So why didn't you fire her when you took over?'

'Because she'd been here twenty years. Because she'd
never have understood. Because it might just have
worked out in the typing pool.' He looked at Cindy
then, his deep blue eyes unsmiling. 'Because I must be
getting soft in my old age, okay?'

'Old age, Zac?' She smiled at him, loving him, wanting him.

'A lot older than you.' He grinned, but there was still no laughter in his eyes. 'Find a replacement, will you? Someone a little less—you know.'

'Shockable?' Cindy laughed and picked up the formally typed letter of resignation. 'So you're not so ruthless after all, eh?'

'I blame you,' he retorted. 'You have a knack of making me behave strangely.'

'You hadn't met me when you made your decision about Miss Druce.'

At that, the smile reached his eyes. 'What did you come in here for, Goldilocks? Were you about to invite me to dinner at your place tonight?'

'No.' And then she lied. 'I just came in to say good morning.'

Cindy went back to her own office. She delegated the job of ringing the employment agency to Alison, then slipped out to make a phone call from a public box. She wanted to make an appointment with her doctor for the following evening, and she didn't want to be overheard.

On the Wednesday morning, Tracy Lynn arrived. It was noon, and she was expected. Cindy went to greet her in the reception area. 'Miss Lynn—I'm Cindy Hetherington, Zac's secretary.' She held out her hand. 'We haven't actually been introduced. Zac's expecting you. And you're bang on time, he'll like that!'

'Tracy, please.' Tracy shook Cindy's hand, her green almond-shaped eyes smiling warmly from a face that was still extremely beautiful—even for close-up photographic work. 'I saw you at the party, Cindy, but I didn't have a chance to talk to you.'

She followed Cindy through reception, towards the offices. 'So what does he want?'

'I'm sorry?'

'Zac. I know him of old. Come on, tell me what he's up to, so I can be forewarned. He's got to have an ulterior motive for inviting me to lunch!'

'I wouldn't know, Tracy.' Cindy was lying in her teeth. 'I was told to book a table at Mario's for twelve-thirty, and that was all I was told.'

'Are you joining us?' Tracy's eyes were lit with amusement and, as Cindy shook her head, she laughed outrageously. 'Then he's definitely up to something if he wants me alone! Do I look okay?'

Cindy couldn't help smiling. She couldn't help liking Tracy Lynn, either. She was vivacious, outgoing—and she wasn't just fishing for a compliment. She stopped in her tracks, looking at Cindy with genuine uncertainty.

The older woman looked no less than stunning in a lemon, low-cut summer dress which was just the sort of thing Cindy would wear. It was simple, beautifully cut, and it suited her. 'Yes,' Cindy smiled. 'More than all right.' In spite of herself, she couldn't prevent the twinge of jealousy that rushed through her at the knowledge that Tracy Lynn might be around for the next few weeks—if Zac had his way.

She handed the model over to Zac, closed the door to his office, and no sooner had she sat down than Alison started questioning her.

'Who was that? Wow!'

'Tracy Lynn,' Cindy said quietly. 'A model—well, ex-model, actually. It seems she retired about six months ago.'

'She's gorgeous! Why did she retire? And why is she seeing Mr Stone? Is it something to do with Germaine Perfumes?'

Cindy shrugged noncommittally. 'It's your turn for an early lunch, Alison. Why don't you go now, while you have the chance?'

Alison switched off her typewriter. 'I'll bet it is.'

It was. Zac wanted to use Tracy Lynn in the television commercial he was planning for Germaine's. The market research was now to hand, and Zac was planning on featuring three different women of different ages and images in the ad. He thought Tracy Lynn would be perfect. So did Greg Halliday. So did Cindy.

It was turned three when Zac came back to the office. Cindy followed him into his room and asked what had happened.

He shook his head. 'She's happy in her retirement. She's absolutely, categorically not interested. She said.'

'What does that mean?' Cindy's relief was squashed by the way Zac had tagged on the last two words.

'It means,' he smiled. 'That I'm taking her to dinner on Friday night, and then maybe she'll say maybe.'

Cindy leaned casually against a filing cabinet. It was against every instinct in her to ask the question, but she just couldn't help herself. 'You and Tracy go back a long way, Zac. Were you lovers, in the past?'

Zac's eyes locked on to hers and held them. 'What's that got to do with anything?'

'Not a thing.' Cindy hated herself for giving in to her curiosity. But it was important to her. Very.

'Yes.' Zac continued to hold her gaze. 'During the last few months at Stone, Mason and Gibbons, we had an affair, though we'd been working together for a couple of years. I used Tracy exclusively on the cosmetics account. Our affair finished when I left the country. Why are you blushing, Cindy? You should have known I wouldn't lie to you. Would you feel better if I had?'

'I'm not blushing.'

On Friday evening, Cindy forced herself to go out. She took herself off to see a play, but she hardly heard a word of it. Jealousy was eating away inside her. And she hated herself for it. It was another new experience for her, and it was negative. But she'd never had reason to feel jealousy before. She'd never loved a man before. Over and over she reminded herself that Zac's date with Tracy was for business reasons.

Over and over again she wondered what they were saying to one another. Were they reminiscing? They were two extremely attractive people—and they'd been lovers.

She walked home from the theatre feeling sick. But she would have felt worse if she'd stayed at home with nothing at all to distract her. As she turned into Priory Court she saw a small BMW parked next to Zac's Jaguar. It didn't belong to one of the residents. There was nothing whatever about the vehicle which could have told Cindy it belonged to Tracy. She just knew that it did. She looked up at the closed curtains of Zac's window and saw a light come on in the living room. They'd just got back from dinner.

What now?

She had known nothing about Zac's arrangements for this evening and even as she hated herself for doing it, she walked towards the cars and touched the bonnet of each of them. They'd used Tracy's car. Zac's engine was cold. Which meant that Tracy had picked him up, or called for him at the agency.

Cindy undressed, but she didn't go to bed. She couldn't. She moved around restlessly in her bedroom. It was eleven-fifteen and she found herself looking at her watch every five minutes. Every fifteen minutes she went and looked out of her window. From the darkness of her living room, she knew, she wouldn't be seen.

At a little after midnight, Tracy's car was gone.

So nothing had happened.

She hoped against hope that Tracy had stood her ground and had not given in to Zac's persuasiveness as far as the Germaine ads were concerned. If Zac told her on Monday morning that Tracy had said yes, or even maybe, she would have to leave Bryant's. She'd have no choice. Nobody knew better than she how persuasive Zac could be. Maybe would mean yes . . . and possibly a great deal more. She couldn't cope with that, with this sick jealousy eating away inside her.

It was the worst weekend of her life. On the Saturday she went to the coast and drove for miles. But she didn't even notice her surroundings. She felt as if she were coming apart at the seams. If she'd known, then, that the decision about her immediate future was to be taken out of her hands, she might have managed to eat something. She might have managed to stop hating herself.

But she didn't know, and things got worse. Late on Sunday evening, Cindy pulled into her parking spot outside the flats. Tracy's car was there. And it was still there at midnight.

At a little after two in the morning, Cindy took a last look from her living room window, and went to bed. The car was still there.

She cried half the night. She took the pills from her dressing table drawer and threw them in the rubbish bin, filled with self-loathing and humiliation. The only thing that prevented her from going insane was the fact that Zac didn't know how close she'd come to having an affair with him.

At a little after eight on the Monday morning, she was jostled from a restless sleep by the jarring of the telephone. She reached for it hurriedly, blindly, unable to bear the noise of it. Part of her mind registered that she'd overslept as she saw the hands of her clock. Then a voice in her head laughed at her for reacting. Her days at Bryant's were numbered. What did it matter if she were late? She would give notice. She would do that because her pride would not allow her to do otherwise. Zac must never know how she felt. Somehow she would work her way through the next two weeks with the dignity and composure inherent in her nature. She would tell Zac that she'd simply made a mistake, that the pace of work was proving to be more than she could cope with. That she wanted to get out before things became impossibly demanding on the Germaine account. It would, after all, be partly true.

'Cindy?'

'Mm . . .? Mummy! What on earth are you ringing at this hour for? I can't chat now, darling, I'm late——'

Cindy's breath was punched from her body by her mother's next words. Her mind blanked out moment-arily as tears started to trickle down her cheeks. She could never have guessed that she would take this news so badly.

'When? . . . And where is he now? . . . And what are his chances?'

She barely gave her mother a chance to answer. She was already out of bed. 'Of course I'm coming! Mummy, how could you think—Let me go. I'll be home as quickly as I can possibly make it!'

She put down the phone and stood, not knowing what to do first. Her father had had a heart attack in the early hours of the morning and was lying in the intensive care unit of a hospital on the outskirts of Manchester.

And Cindy had never forgiven him.

She broke down, sobbing as she had never sobbed before. But she was on the move even as she did so. With trembling hands she stuffed clothes into two suitcases. Then she washed and dressed.

Only then did she remember Zac.

She flew to the window, wondering whether he'd left for the office. Tracy's car was there, but Zac's wasn't. She snatched up the phone and dialled Bryant's number, her hands clenching and unclenching as she waited to be put through to her boss. 'Zac, listen. I have to go home at once—my father's had a heart attack. It's bad, Zac. I have——'

She heard the sharp intake of breath at the other end of the line. 'Of course, of course,' he said hurriedly. 'God, Cindy, I'm so sorry . . . Ring me when you can. Let me know how he's doing.'

Cindy got out of Priory Court as quickly as she could, hampered by her suitcases. She'd just flung them in the boot of her car when someone tapped her on the shoulder. She turned to see Tracy Lynn, looking a little nonplussed at seeing Cindy, but smiling, as friendly as ever.

'Cindy? I thought it was you! Are you looking for Zac? He left about half an hour ago.' She laughed girlishly. 'I'm afraid we overslept this morning! But he'll be at the office by now, if you——'

'I wasn't looking for Zac.' How Cindy didn't bite her head off, she'd never know. But the feeling of nausea churning inside her seemed to have robbed her of the necessary energy. 'I live here, too, as a matter of fact. Excuse me, Tracy, I'm in a hurry.'

The two women got into their cars and Cindy pulled out first, her eyes swimming with tears. Only then did she question her decision to drive to the north. But it would be the fastest way. If she took a train, she'd have to get to Euston first ... She took hold of herself mentally, acknowledging that the situation would not be helped by her own hysteria.

The rush hour traffic was chronic, even on the motorway. It was only when she left the M1 to join the M6 that Cindy was able to put her foot down. She drove fast, but carefully, her reactions automatic. In a corner of her mind she could hear her mother's voice, asking whether Cindy would come home at once. Asking. How incredibly, desperately sad it was that her mother had needed to ask. What an appalling thing that was! But she couldn't blame her mother, she could blame only herself. The strain between Cindy and her father had been tangible for the past ten years, and a constant source of sadness to her mother.

Cindy blinked against a fresh bout of tears. Dear Lord, she prayed, let him live! Let him live to be a hundred. Let him live to enjoy his retirement. Let him live that I may put things right between us.

At the dictate of common sense she pulled into a service area and forced herself to drink a cup of coffee. Not that she wanted it; it was just in an effort to halt, once and for all, the tears which were blinding her vision.

At a little after noon, she drew to a halt in the hospital car park. She saw the grey Bentley, the family car, parked a few spaces away. Then she saw George Butterworth, the chauffeur-cum-head gardener, walking hurriedly towards her.

'Miss Cynthia!' George smiled warmly and something

inside Cindy snapped with relief. 'It's all right, miss. Your father's holding his own. I'll take you to Lady Hetherington.'

Cindy smiled and nodded, not trusting herself to speak. She patted the arm George extended to her and let her hand rest there, grateful to him. He and his wife, who worked as housekeeper, had been around for as long as Cindy could remember.

George escorted her to the private wing of the hospital and opened the door to a waiting room which was painted stark white, closing the door quietly after him as he left Cindy alone with her mother.

Lady Hetherington was sitting erect, quietly composed, as always. Her greying fair hair was as neat as ever, swept into a French roll with not a hair out of place. She was a petite woman, much shorter than any of her three daughters, perfectly groomed and possessed of an air of dignity which sometimes obscured her warmth. In the latter respect she and Cindy were very much mother and daughter. But her face crumpled slightly as she saw Cindy.

'Mummy!' Cindy threw her arms around her and lowered herself on to the couch. It was one of two, together with two straight-backed chairs, which filled the waiting room to capacity. 'Why are you alone? Where are my sisters? How come——'

'It's all right, darling. I'm fine, just fine. Felicity was with me until about ten minutes ago. She's gone back to the house. Jonathan says there's no point in our waiting here, but I'm not going home until I hear something positive.'

'Jonathan? Thank heavens!' Cindy sagged with relief. Jonathan Trent was an old friend of the family and an eminent doctor. Her father couldn't be in better hands. 'What about Paula? Has she been told?'

Lady Hetherington shook her head. 'She flew to California last night with her husband and the boys. We shan't be able to contact her until this evening.'

'Let's hope we'll have better news by then.'

Cindy's mother was still holding on to her hand. 'Darling, thank you for coming so quickly. It's been such a shock——'

Before Cindy could reply, Jonathan Trent came in, but he was cautious with his reassurances. 'Cindy, it's good to see you. I only wish it were under different circumstances.' He turned to Cindy's mother, motioning her to sit down again. 'There's no change, Pamela. I want you to go home. There's no point whatever in your sitting here. You know I'll ring you if I've anything to report.'

'I'm not going anywhere, Jonathan.' Lady Hetherington sat down again.

'When can we see him?' Cindy was on her feet now and the doctor slipped an arm around her shoulder.

'Not today, I'm afraid.'

'Is he going to pull through, Jonathan?' She could see the lines of strain around the doctor's face, his hesitation before he answered.

'It was bad, Cindy, but I've seen worse. Now, your father's as strong as an ox, he's been in good health and apart from that he's remarkably stubborn.' He smiled thinly. 'I think he'll pull through. But we must take this as a severe warning. He'll have to take things very easily in the future. And I shall be keeping a keen eye on him.'

'You *think* he'll pull through?' She hardly heard anything else. 'Is he awake? Can I go in and see him? Please, Jonathan!'

'No. To both questions.' He smiled to soften the blow. 'I'll have some tea sent in to you.'

Cindy and her mother sat quietly for over an hour, comforting one another without words. When Jonathan returned they could both tell, instantly, that he was feeling more confident. 'He's asking for you, Pamela. He's going to be all right.'

Cindy was on her feet instantly but the doctor put a restraining hand on her shoulder. 'Just a minute, young lady. He's asking for your mother. I'm going to allow you precisely one minute with him, Pamela. On the condition that you promise to go home afterwards.'

'All right.' Lady Hetherington managed a smile, her voice weak with relief.

'And when can I see him?'

'Tomorrow night. For five minutes, perhaps. Bring your mother and your sister at seven o'clock, and ask for me.'

They drove back to Cheshire in convoy, Cindy with her mother in the passenger seat and George Butterworth ahead of them in the Bentley. They found Felicity in the drawing room, standing by the French windows, smoking nervously.

'Hello, Cindy. Mummy—is there any change?' Felicity walked hastily toward them and sank wearily into a chair when she was told that her father was going to live. She had driven up from her home in Staffordshire that morning and would be staying for a few days, she said.

'I'm going to my room.' Lady Hetherington didn't bother to sit. 'Tell Mrs B. I don't want to be disturbed, Flick.'

'What about having something to eat, Mummy? You had no breakfast, no lunch——'

'I'll be down for dinner at the usual time,' her mother said quietly.

When Lady Hetherington had left the room, Cindy got the details of what had happened in the early hours from her sister. Felicity was the middle one of the three daughters and she and Cindy had never got on terribly well. And that had nothing to do with Flick's eight years' seniority, because Cindy got on extremely well with the eldest of them, Paula.

'What about Charles?' Cindy asked about her sister's husband. 'Will he drive up this evening?'

'No. He's bogged down with work. Besides, he's perfectly capable of being left for a few days. I want to stay here until I'm satisfied that Daddy's going to recover fully.'

That, at least, was something they had in common.

'You might have hung on at the hospital,' Cindy

admonished. 'I found my mother sitting there by herself, looking ghastly. Why didn't you wait till I got there at least?'

Felicity stubbed out her cigarette rather crossly. 'Because I knew you'd be there soon. Because I'd vomited twice. Because I couldn't bear to sit in that horrible room, waiting. Just waiting.'

'Are you ill? Or was it the——'

'I'm pregnant,' Flick shrugged, seeming neither pleased nor displeased over her news.

'Oh, congratulations!' Cindy's pleasure was evident. Her sister had waited a long time for this. After eleven years of marriage, everyone had long since decided it wasn't going to happen.

Mrs Butterworth came in with a jug of coffee and three cups. Inasmuch as she was painfully thin, Mrs B. was not everyone's idea of a cook/housekeeper. But she was a wizard in the kitchen and she'd been running the Hetherington household more than well for many years.

'Miss Cynthia, it's nice to see you again, though I certainly didn't expect it to be so soon after your summer visit. But George has told me the news. Sir Robert's going to be all right. Thank heaven for that!' She put down the tray, chattering more than was usual in her relief. 'Where's Lady Hetherington?'

'She doesn't want coffee or anything to eat, Mrs B.' Flick held up a hand as the housekeeper started to protest. 'She will be down for dinner, though, so please don't fuss.'

Dinner was a solemn affair in spite of the doctor's reassurance. Neither Lady Hetherington nor her daughters would relax fully until they saw the patient's improvement for themselves, although the atmosphere relaxed somewhat when Jonathan telephoned at nine o'clock with a progress report and an assurance that it would not be necessary to bring Paula and her family home from her holiday in America.

Paula had been contacted, and Cindy put through a further call to relay the latest news. After that she went to her room and flopped exhaustedly on to her bed. She had slept very little the previous evening, and she was to sleep even less tonight.

Her mind, now, seemed to be split into two separate compartments, each of which was battling for her fullest attention. Every time she closed her eyes she saw a mental image of her father lying in a white hospital bed in a white room, with a white-coated doctor standing by his side.

Then, like slides on a projector, the picture would be replaced by another on which there was also a bed, a larger bed in a room she had never seen, and on it there was Zac and a dark-haired beauty making love. Zac was holding Tracy Lynn in his arms, his deep blue eyes looking smilingly, intimately into hers, just as he had looked into Cindy's eyes . . .

For as long as she lived she would be grateful that she had never known the fullest extent of Zac's lovemaking. For as long as she lived she would be grateful she had not numbered among his affairs. Meaningless affairs.

Perhaps, with Tracy Lynn, it wouldn't be meaningless. They were picking up where they'd left off two years ago. Maybe Zac was in love with her, maybe that was why he invited her to Bryant's party. Maybe that was why it was she he wanted for the Germaine ad when he could have taken his choice of a hundred other models—so he could pick up where he'd left off.

There again, maybe it was just sex. Maybe Zac had turned to Tracy for the fulfilment Cindy had denied him. Oh, how quickly he had done that! How it served to demonstrate the nothingness of his feelings for Cindy.

She tried to tell herself she didn't care. She didn't care that Zac felt less than nothing for her. Didn't care that he'd made love to Tracy in a flat right next door to her own, so soon after Paris . . . Paris . . . Another woman . . .

Cindy pulled the bedding closer around her, curling

up tightly into the embryonic attitude as if the warm softness of her bed would serve as a womb to protect her from all the hurts which life could inflict, so many of which had assailed her within the space of one day. But she did care. She *cared*. She cared because she loved Zac Stone regardless of anything and everything. But she would never see him again. Not for an instant. She had made her escape from him quicker than she had expected to, and while she desperately regretted the circumstances which had brought that about, it was an enormous relief to her.

It meant it was over. Cleanly, swiftly. Now she might start to heal, to become whole again.

If only the pain would stop.

CHAPTER ELEVEN

'CINDY . . . I wasn't expecting . . . It was good of you to come. Is your mother outside?'

Cindy forced herself to smile as she approached the bed. It was an effort to force the words past the constriction in her throat. 'Yes. With Flick. They . . . they let me come in first.' She sat close to her father, determined not to let him see how the sight of him affected her. He looked ten years older than he had only a couple of months ago, in June—when she had found his company a strain. His bushy hair looked greyer than ever. His face, normally jovial-looking and ruddy, was tense, almost as white as the pillows he was propped up against.

And then a momentary silence hung between them as Cindy's vision blurred. She sat perfectly still, struggling for control, frightened lest she give him any kind of stress.

'You know what this means, don't you?' Sir Robert's voice reflected his attempt at lightness, but his eyes closed wearily even as he spoke. 'It means my golfing days are over.'

'Oh, Daddy!' Cindy leaned closer to him, slipping her hand into his as the tears brimmed over and spilled on to her cheeks. Her father's eyes closed again, but Cindy felt his fingers tighten around her hand. It had been a long, long time since she had called him Daddy. That, and the way he continued to hold her hand tightly, was all they needed to say to each other really. For the time being, at least.

'Not necessarily,' she whispered. 'Not necessarily.'

'It doesn't matter anyway,' he smiled. 'There's always the putting green.'

'Yes, there's always the putting green.'

'How long can you stay?'

'Five minutes.'

'No, I mean at home—in Cheshire?' He chuckled as Cindy laughed far more than was called for.

'As long as I like. I'm—in between jobs. Now, I must get out of here or else Jonathan will chase me. Mummy will be with you in a moment. And Flick's twitching to see you, naturally.'

'One at a time, eh?' Sir Robert grimaced at the thought. 'He's a real stickler, old Jonathan.'

'And he's quite right.' Cindy broke the contact of their hands reluctantly. 'I'll see you tomorrow.'

She visited alone the following day, having arranged with her mother and sister that they would go to the hospital in the evenings and she would go during the afternoon. That way her father would have two visits instead of one. Jonathan was agreeable—provided they didn't stay too long.

Having reported to her mother and sister that Sir Robert looked a little better, still white but a little less tired, Cindy went up to her room to make an attempt at sleeping. She had just got undressed when Felicity barged in without bothering to knock.

'Cindy?'

'I'm in the bathroom. I'm going to bed for a couple of hours. I told you. What do you want?' Cindy emerged from the bathroom to find her sister sitting on her bed, smoking. 'You might have brought an ashtray with you if you intended to smoke in my room. Anyway, shouldn't you give that up now you're pregnant?'

Flick tutted, walked into the bathroom and came back without the cigarette. 'Typical! If you were pregnant, you'd do everything by the book, wouldn't you?'

'Actually, yes. What do you want?'

'There was a phone call for you while you were at the hospital. I forgot to tell you just now.' She draped herself into a chair, mischief evident in her eyes. 'From a man—a man with a gorgeous voice. I can only describe it as . . . gravelly.'

Cindy's stomach contracted.

'Your employer, I believe.'

'And?' She kept her voice nonchalant as she got into bed, avoiding her sister's eyes.

Flick raised an eyebrow. 'Does he look as attractive as he sounds?'

'For heaven's sake——'

'Well?'

Cindy swallowed hard, hoping it didn't show. 'Yes, as a matter of fact he does.'

'Then he can park his shoes under my bed any time!' Flick laughed outrageously. 'You must introduce me to him at once!'

Cindy shot her a contemptuous look. 'In the circumstances, that's a very strange thing to say.'

'Because I'm married or because I'm pregnant?'

'Both. You and Charles are happy enough, aren't you?'

'Happy enough . . .' Flick repeated the words slowly. 'I wonder what that means, exactly. Let's say there's room for improvement. Still, the baby might improve things . . . And there again, it might not.' She tossed back her hair, hair much darker than Cindy's—though her eyes were very similar. Then she stood and smoothed the skirt over her slender hips. Cindy wanted to shake her even as she realised her sister wasn't keeping her waiting deliberately.

She cleared her throat. 'What did he say, Mr Stone?'

'Zac,' Flick amended, pointedly, 'was asking about our father. What's he like, Cindy? Have you got something going with him?'

'Of course not.' She was losing patience, but she didn't want to protest too much.

'Of course not!' The older girl shrugged, not doubting Cindy's word for a moment. 'I think I'll have to knit a man for you. You'd better write down your list of specifications. You've always been faddy, haven't you? I remember——'

'Flick, please. I came up here to sleep.'

'All right, all right. There's nothing else to tell. He didn't ask for you to call him back. He didn't say he'd call back. He said he was sorry to trouble me, but he was anxious to know how Sir Robert was, and that he was very glad to hear he was out of danger and making progress. Okay, madam?' As she flounced out, Cindy put her hands up to her cheeks. They were hot.

She would have to write to Zac at once—before he telephoned again. There was no way she wanted to speak to him. It would be so much easier to explain her reasons for leaving in a letter. He couldn't protest to a letter. If he wanted to protest at all, that was. She would tell him, simply, that she wouldn't be coming back to London for quite a time, that he'd better get a replacement straight away, that she could no longer cope with the pace of work, in any case.

She wrote the letter that evening, keeping it as brief and succinct as possible. And she posted it before the last collection. With luck, it would reach London the following day.

By Friday there was no doubt that the letter had reached its destination. Two days was certainly enough time. Cindy waited anxiously for a phone call she would try to avoid at all costs. She spent all morning in the grounds of the house, which were extensive, so she might be out of reach if a call came.

But there was no call.

By Monday evening she relaxed slightly. Zac wouldn't phone now. And so much for the idea that he might protest over Cindy's resignation. Of course she knew his attitude. He would shrug and remind himself, as she had heard him do, that nobody is indispensable, nobody is irreplaceable.

Except him, of course. He was indispensable to Bryant's and he was irreplaceable as far as Cindy was concerned. There would never be anyone else for her. There was no one like him. She had never loved a man before Zac, and there was no one else for her.

The following morning, she woke up with a screaming headache and a streaming nose. She spent the rest of the week in bed, unable to visit the hospital. Flick had gone back to Staffordshire, but her mother was visiting the hospital twice daily. Sir Robert was making remarkably good progress, improving daily.

Cindy was on her feet again by the time her birthday came around on the twelfth of September, and it was on that evening, over a very nice meal prepared in her honour, that her mother told her Sir Robert would be coming home within the next few days.

'Jonathan told me this evening.' Pamela Hetherington looked almost excited. 'He's been so good, you know. I really must——' She broke off suddenly, looking at her daughter as if she hadn't seen her for years. 'Darling, are you all right? Are you sure you've got rid of that 'flu?'

'It wasn't 'flu, Mummy.' Cindy perked up immediately because she didn't want her mother scrutinising too closely. 'It's wonderful news about Daddy, isn't it? He'll have to take it very, very easy.'

'I know—I've been warned. He'll have to cut his brandy consumption drastically.'

'Totally, I should have thought.'

'Ideally, yes, but do you think he will?'

'Not for a minute!' Cindy laughed, but her mother was not easily distracted.

'There's something wrong, Cindy. With you. I've been so frantic about your father that I haven't stopped to notice until now. What is it, darling? It's something more than a cold, isn't it?'

'I—it's nothing. I haven't been sleeping too well, that's all.'

She knew without doubt that her letter to Zac had not gone astray. She knew that because she had received a birthday card from Alison in which there was a letter saying how sorry Alison was that Cindy wouldn't be returning to Bryant's, and how much she would miss her. But there had been not a word from Zac. He hadn't even bothered to acknowledge the letter of resignation.

'Which means,' her mother said softly, 'that you don't want to talk about it.'

Cindy put her knife and fork down, nodding briefly. 'That was super. It was sweet of Mrs B. to make something special for me. I must thank her . . .' Her mind drifted. 'I'm sorry? What did you say?'

'I said Happy Birthday, darling.' Lady Hetherington handed her a small, beautifully wrapped package. From me and Daddy . . . . Cindy, you know how pleased I am—about you and your father—but I'm wondering how long you intend to stay. You know I love your being here, but what about this job of yours? From what you told me over the phone, it sounds as if Mr Stone is hardly the type who——'

'I've left,' Cindy cut in. 'I'm sorry, I should have mentioned that before. I—I've left Bryant's. It was—well, you were always telling me I worked too hard. And how unnecessary it was.'

Her mother inclined her head slightly, her small hands spread before her. It was her way of saying she'd leave the subject alone. Unless and until Cindy wanted to talk about it.

Grateful, for her birthday gift as well as her mother's understanding, Cindy got up and hugged her. 'Let's go into the drawing room, shall we? How about a game of Scrabble?'

It was rather like being young again, really young. Before things had changed between herself and her father. Before she was thirteen. The huge old house had a happy atmosphere now that its master was due to come home. Nothing seemed to change, apart from the decorations. The grounds were immaculate, the gardens beautiful in all seasons. Especially now, where September roses were still flourishing in the rose garden.

Cindy loved the house, with its antiques and its family portraits and its richly coloured carpets, old and cherished. But she wouldn't want to live in something as big as this herself, any more than she would choose to decorate and furnish the way her parents had. It was too old, a little austere, a little too quiet. Soon, she knew, she would grow bored with it. As always. It was nice to come home and it was nice to go away again— back to her own flat.

But what now? She wouldn't be returning to her own flat. That was out of the question. She wouldn't even go there to collect her things, to remove her furniture. She would pay someone to do that for her. Money really did have its uses at times. In the meantime, she'd send off a cheque for the next quarter's rent and give notice to the agents that she was vacating.

Perhaps she'd buy a small house. Somewhere on the outskirts of the capital, close enough that she'd be able to commute to her new place of work. She would have a garden, then, in which to keep herself busy at weekends. And she'd take up her evening classes again. One thing was for sure—she couldn't stay in Cheshire for ever. She was well aware that she was using the place as a sanctuary, that she'd have to sort herself out sooner or later.

By early October, after a couple of weeks' bedrest, Cindy's father was taking daily strolls around the grounds, venturing farther and longer each day. Cindy went with him, just as she used to during the holidays of her childhood. Sometimes George would accompany them, or one of the other gardeners, and they would inspect together everything which grew. Sir Robert had taught Cindy everything she knew about flowers and plants, though he had rarely had time for gardening in the past.

They got caught in a sudden shower one afternoon towards the end of the month, when, needless to say, they couldn't have been farther from shelter. They were on the edge of the woods which skirted one side of the estate, picking their way through a carpet of gold and amber leaves which quickly turned soggy.

'Don't fuss, Cindy!' Sir Robert laughed at his daughter's concern. 'I won't melt if I get wet.'

She looked up at him. He was a tall man, tall and stocky. And he still appeared to be as strong as an ox. The colour was back in his face, the tension eased, and he was looking more like his sixty-one years than he had several weeks ago.

'Go on with what you were saying,' he urged. 'You were telling me how much thought goes into the packaging of a product, the effect of colour and shape.'

'That's right.' Cindy chatted on while they strolled. She did, after all, know a lot about advertising and the psychology behind it. 'Daddy,' she said at length, 'are you really interested in all this? I mean, you've never asked me before.'

'You've never given me the chance before,' he said quietly. She nodded, biting her lip. There was no answer to that.

'Besides,' he went on, 'I wouldn't have asked if I weren't interested. Anyway, when are you going home to start looking for another job? With your experience, you'll have no trouble finding a position in another agency.'

'I—I don't know when I'm leaving. I'm trying to decide what to do. I'll . . . have to do something to fill my time.'

'How about settling down and giving me a couple more grandchildren?' Sir Robert was smiling but he was half serious. 'That'd fill your time!'

Cindy kicked at the leaves and made no comment. She looked up at the naked branches of the trees, watching a solitary sparrow hopping from branch to branch as they walked together slowly, as if it were listening in on their conversation. 'I'll probably look for something which will be a complete change. I—won't go back into advertising.'

'That doesn't make much sense! Cindy, I'm not at all clear why you left Bryant's. I mean, it sounds so interesting and that boss of your seems like a remarkable sort of chap.'

'He is.' She had spoken of Zac, inevitably. How could she not, when her father had been asking about her work? 'He's brilliant,' she added quietly. 'And very, very talented.'

Sir Robert looked at her quickly. 'Stone,' he said thoughtfully. 'Zachariah Stone. Am I likely to know his family?'

'No. Zac comes from a small village in Wales—I can't even pronounce its name. He's the last in a long line of coalminers.'

'Indeed? Then he must be remarkable. He wasn't exactly born with a silver spoon, was he?'

'Not exactly. But he's very . . . ambitious.'

'And you're in love with him. Ah, Cindy . . .' her father took hold of her arm and linked it through his own, 'I must be getting old! I've only just realised what the trouble is.'

Cindy let out a long, slow breath. 'And I'm in love with him. No, I *was* in love with him.'

'And now you've left. You had an affair, I take it?'

She met her father's eyes steadily. 'Is this the clever lawyer probing, or is it my father?'

'The man,' he said quietly. 'Just the man.'

She squeezed his arm, understanding precisely what he was saying.

'Cindy, you said you're in love with Zac. Then you immediately put it in the past tense. Did you justify your affair with him by telling yourself you loved him?'

She smiled wryly, her eyes lit with amusement and admiration. Her father was far cleverer than she; she should have known he would be one step ahead of her. 'No, I didn't. I didn't need to justify myself. I went to bed with Zac before I realised I was in love with him— at least, before I'd admitted it to myself. I did it because I wanted him physically. So at that stage it was—just sex.' Her laughter then was brittle, hollow, self-deprecating. 'Just sex. That was something, a notion, I'd always thought of and spoken of with distaste in the past. That's one of the reasons I remained a virgin for so long. That, plus the fact that there was a switch inside me which hadn't been thrown until, until . . .'

'Until you met Zac.'

'Until I met Zac. So you see, I understood the power of sex only intellectually in the past. Which is not the same as having personal experience. I thought of it only in terms of it being a troublemaker—to me, very easy to resist.'

'Only in terms of it being a troublemaker?' Sir Robert looked at her gravely. 'How very sad, that you thought only along those lines. I—I'm afraid I'm responsible for that.'

'No.' Cindy spread her hands in a gesture of helplessness. 'I'm a mature woman, Daddy. I should have changed my thinking a long time ago. I don't—I can't—sit in judgment any more.' Quietly she added, 'It's important that I actually say this to you.'

Her father stood still, meeting her eyes. 'I appreciate that—you'll never know how much. And I'm glad your thinking has changed. For your own sake, I mean. Come on, let's sit down for a while.'

The shower had stopped, and the only place to sit was on the clean-cut stump of a huge old oak tree. Cindy pulled her coat more closely around her, looking quickly at her father to make sure he wasn't getting overtired.

How good it was to be able to talk to him, of all people, at such a level. A few months ago she would never have believed it possible. Yet here she was, and finding it remarkably easy, too. 'But it all went wrong, Daddy, with me and Zac. It was in early August. We were in Paris on a business trip when we . . . But it all went wrong.' Almost defiantly she tossed back her head and looked at her father directly. 'I'm still a virgin, Daddy. What do you think of that? I'm twenty-four years old and I'm still a virgin.'

He chuckled. 'Are you bragging about it?'

'No. I'm appalled by it.'

He laughed loudly then. But he never did say what he

thought about it. 'But how were things when you left London? Did you have a fight? I mean, what happened between Paris and your coming here?'

It was a good question. Cindy picked up a damp twig and fiddled with it absently, her mind drifting back over the weeks. Zac, and Zac alone, had been in control, all along. He could have taken her the first night he'd kissed her. He'd known that at the time. But she certainly hadn't—not then. And when he had told her of his intentions, she still didn't believe it would happen. She thought she could escape him. What a stupid idea that had been . . . And then there was Paris. Two weeks later there was Tracy Lynn. But why? Why had he taken up with her when he knew full well that Cindy couldn't resist him? Perhaps he felt the challenge had been met? But it hadn't! And that was something about Zac which just didn't make sense . . .

'Cindy?'

'I dithered.' She shrugged. 'Zac didn't—I vacillated between—Oh, damn! Paula must have arrived. Look!'

In the distance she could see her sister's thirteen- and fourteen-year-old sons coming towards them at a steady trot, waving energetically. In the few remaining moments of privacy she said, 'Anyway, this is where it gets a little complex, Daddy. I decided to leave Bryant's. I decided to have an affair with Zac and just enjoy it for what it would be. I decided to stay, and do nothing. I decided I couldn't leave him, because I loved him. And I decided an affair with him was the last thing I wanted. I dithered! See what I mean?'

Sir Robert grunted, shaking his head. 'Because by then you wanted much more. My poor darling! You've had an awful time, and I'm sorry. One thing's very clear, however, from all you've told me. You're still very much in love with Zac—very much. And it's high time you went back to London and sorted things out with him. Go and talk to him, Cindy. Stop using me as an excuse to stay here—and go home. Get on with your life.'

He said it gently, nicely, and before she had time to tell him there was nothing to sort out, that Zac didn't even care enough about her to acknowledge a letter, that he'd found someone else even before she'd left, her nephews were within earshot. The conversation ended abruptly as Cindy immediately took control and made sure the youngsters didn't get too boisterous.

During the next couple of days, the weekend, Cindy diverted her nephews by taking them out to the cinema and for a meal. They were good boys, and Paula certainly knew how to keep them in check, but Cindy was anxious that their youthful exuberance might prove too much for their grandfather. She was probably being obsessive, she realised, but having found her father again after so many years, she dreaded to think what another heart attack might do to him.

Jonathan Trent was keeping a watchful eye on Sir Robert, too. He had called regularly at the house and had twice personally driven his patient to the hospital in order that he might do a more thorough examination.

But her father had been right; she was using him as an excuse to stay. When October slipped into November she realised, with a shock, that she had been at home for two months. Two months. And yes, she was bored, but she was also safe.

And what incentive was there for her to leave?

She was floating, just as she'd been when she was eighteen. She was so much more experienced, so much more enlightened, yet once again she didn't know what to do with her life.

Her parents just let her be. Over the next few weeks Sir Robert said nothing more about her going back to London. Neither did her mother. They didn't press her, one way or another. They wouldn't urge her to leave any more than they would urge her to stay. And she loved them for it.

CHAPTER TWELVE

TOWARDS the end of November, however, Cindy was feeling a lot better. She started to heal, was no longer hurting every time she thought back. Her entire perspective had changed. Looking back on her last couple of months in London was no longer painful. She felt detached, as if she were looking at the situation from a great distance, as one might see something through the wrong end of a telescope. The details were sharp, clear, but she could stand back from it now and see it for what it was—just a chapter of her life which had passed.

On the last Friday of the month, over lunch, she told her parents she was leaving. 'I've just telephoned the porter at Priory Court and he's making arrangements for a removal company to clear out my flat one day next week. I've sent him my key. Everything will be put into storage for me until I find somewhere else to live.'

Her mother and father exchanged looks. Worried looks. 'Oh, it's all right,' Cindy smiled. 'For some time now I've been thinking of buying a house on the outskirts of London. I'll be much nearer the countryside but near enough to get into town. I shall find myself a new job immediately after New Year. I'll be leaving next Friday. I'm staying another week so I can be here for your birthday, Daddy.'

Sir Robert grunted, looking down at his plate and obviously restraining himself not to say anything.

Her mother was less controlled. 'But, darling, it's December next week. What—what will you do with yourself until New Year?'

'I shall go to Bournemouth, as usual.' Cindy hadn't spent Christmas with her parents for the past five years.

It was too much to cope with. *All* the family gathered at the big house—her sisters, cousins, several aunts and uncles, and it had never been her scene. She had always spent Christmas with an old school friend, a very dear friend, in Bournemouth, and she saw no reason to change her routine this year.

'Oh.' Lady Hetherington looked quite disappointed. 'I thought this year might be different. I mean, now you and Daddy——'

'Now, Pamela.' Sir Robert shot her a warning look. 'We mustn't interfere.' To his daughter he said, 'You do whatever you feel like doing, Cindy. Will you go straight to Bournemouth from here?'

'Yes. I've already phoned Emma and David. Emma was delighted—you know how she is. She said come when you like and stay as long as you like. Actually, she'll be glad of the company because her husband has to go to Japan on business in the middle of December. He won't be back until a couple of days before Christmas.'

It would be quiet at Emma's. They would go for long walks along the sea front and they would natter about old times, as they always did. At Christmas they would be joined only by David's mother. There would be no madding crowd, nothing for Cindy to do but decide where to start looking for a house and what sort of job she would take.

Mrs Butterworth came in with a steamed pudding, and lunch continued pleasantly. Nothing else was said to Cindy about her plans.

'Now, Daddy, what on earth am I going to buy you for your birthday next week? I've been thinking about it for days and I haven't been inspired. You seem to have everything.'

'As a matter of fact,' Sir Robert laughed, 'I haven't. I'll tell you exactly what I want—a new camera.'

Cindy's mother suppressed a smile as she looked at her. Her father's request was of no help at all—she and her mother had already shopped for the camera he wanted over a week ago. That was his wife's present, so Cindy would have to start thinking all over again.

'I'll see what I can do,' Cindy said noncommittally. 'Shall we go into town on Wednesday, Mummy? There's one or two other bits of shopping I'd like to do at the same time.'

'Yes, darling, that'll be nice.'

'Who else is coming to dinner on Thursday?'

'Just Jonathan Trent and his wife.' Sir Robert waved a dismissive arm. 'No one else. I don't want a room full of people making a fuss, just because I've reached the grand old age of sixty-two.'

'Surely Paula's coming?'

'No. She's got her in-laws staying this week. And Flick isn't coming, either. She's not feeling too well.'

The conversation changed then, to Flick and the baby she was expecting. Each time Cindy had seen her sister she seemed happier about her pregnancy, though she wasn't having an easy time of it.

Cindy went shopping alone on the Wednesday. It was a foul day, freezing cold and pouring with sleet. The weather put her mother right off the idea of a trip into town, but Cindy had no choice about going. She'd left it until the last minute and she had to come up with something for her father's birthday the next day.

She took her own car into town, seeing no reason to keep the chauffeur hanging around for hours while she went from shop to shop. As a reward for her efforts she called in at a hairdresser's and had her hair trimmed and blow-dried—which was a complete waste of time, because she got wet coming out of the shop and her hair was curling uncontrollably by the time she was half way home.

As she turned into the long, sweeping driveway of her parents' house in the middle of the afternoon, Cindy's foot jerked on the accelerator and her breath left her body in a short, frightened gasp. At the top of the drive, parked directly in front of the house, there was a black car. Even from a distance there was no mistaking the sleek and graceful line of it. It was a Jaguar.

She stood on her brakes, looking in front of her as if she had come up against an invisible wall she would never be able to get past. Even as her hands started trembling she was telling herself not to be so stupid. There was more than one black Jaguar in the world. There was no reason to suppose . . . It must belong to one of her father's friends. But whom?

Cindy's car stalled. She looked stupidly at the steering wheel, at the keys, her mind frozen so that she had no idea how to set the car in motion again. She felt utterly sick as she realised that nothing had changed, nothing at all. So much for her healing time! So much for her detachedness!

She didn't know who the black Jaguar belonged to. But she knew for certain who it *didn't* belong to. With that in mind she made an effort to start her own car and continued slowly up the drive, her windscreen wipers beating a steady rhythm as they coped with the downpour. The sleet had turned to rain, heavy rain which looked as if it wouldn't let up for a long time.

Only when she turned off the drive and on to the gravel sweeping round the front of the house was she able to read the number-plate of the Jaguar. She came to an abrupt halt, switched off her engine and just sat, unable to move. All her energy seemed to have cut off, as the power of her engine had cut off. She reached for the handle of her door, but her fingers wouldn't obey her. Her hand fell limply on to her lap.

What did he want of her? *Why had he come here?*

Frantically she looked around, at the trees, at the garages beyond the house, at the bushes. Her instinct was to run away and hide even as she knew she had no choice but to go indoors. She didn't want to see him. She didn't want to be plunged back in time, back into the torment which was her love for him.

But it was too late. Just seeing the black car had told her that. Even before she knew who the car belonged to her body had turned to pulp, a mass of raw emotion she no longer had control over. She was, then, in precisely

the state she had been in on the morning she had left
Priory Court. Filled with nausea at the knowledge that
the man she loved had spent the night, perhaps the
weekend, with another woman. Consumed by fear over
what she might have to face at the end of her journey.

The journey from the car to the house was a short
one, but Cindy took each step of it with dread. She
prayed that she would manage, somehow, to hide her
feelings. She had once been labelled as cool . . . Dear
Lord, she prayed, let me behave that way now. Don't
let him see how much I care.

Through the closed drawing-room door she heard her
mother's laughter and then her voice, far more
animated than usual, 'Oh, I agree with you entirely.
Please—won't you call me Pamela?'

And then there was the rumble of laughter, deep,
warm and oh, so familiar! 'Only if you promise not to
call me Zachariah.'

Cindy started as she caught sight of herself in the hall
mirror. She couldn't go in there looking as she did. Her
face was white, her lips colourless, and her dark brown
eyes reflected her panic. She heard her father's voice,
then her mother's, then the door of the drawing room
swung open and her mother stepped into the hall.

Lady Hetherington closed the door swiftly but
silently as her eyes alighted on her daughter. 'Cindy, for
heaven's sake . . . don't worry. Darling, you're as white
as a sheet!'

'What does he want?' she said lifelessly.

'Well, he wants to talk to you, I suppose.' Her
mother reached out to touch Cindy's cheeks as if she
would bring back some colour. 'Put some lipstick on,'
she said firmly. 'And get hold of yourself.' Then she
smiled reassuringly. 'I know how you feel, darling . . .
Oh, yes, I do. I'm not too old to have forgotten this sort
of emotion, you know.'

Cindy lowered herself on to a chair and took her
compact from her bag, not willing to make any
comment.

'I find him absolutely charming!' her mother said it as if it would help matters. 'Now go in there, Cindy. I'll be back in a moment. I'm just going to tell Mrs B. there'll be one more for dinner this evening.'

'*What?*' Cindy's voice was a coarse whisper. 'You haven't asked him to dine with us? Mummy, what are you thinking about!'

Lady Hetherington looked nonplussed. 'My dear girl, when someone calls at my home after driving two hundred miles in the pouring rain, I wouldn't dream of not asking them to stay for a meal.' And with that, she vanished.

As much as Cindy was prepared for it, it was still a shock coming face to face with him. If anything, he looked more attractive than ever. He was wearing plain slacks and a polo-neck sweater in black cashmere. He stood as she entered, tall, lithe and powerful as he inclined his dark head towards her, just as if he'd seen her only yesterday.

'Hello, Cindy.' The deep blue eyes told her nothing. They were shuttered, yet she knew he was probing her face, her mind, even as his face remained impassive. Then he smiled broadly, and Cindy's heart beat even faster because it was a beautiful sight . . . and because she feared he might know more than she wanted him to know.

'Hello, Zac.' Even as she said it, her eyes went to those of her father. But she knew he would have said nothing to Zac; she knew that without doubt.

'Well, this is quite a surprise, isn't it, Cindy?' Sir Robert's voice was just right, not too jovial, not too casual.

'Quite a surprise.' She sat opposite Zac as he resumed his place on the settee. Her father was in an armchair adjacent to the settee. 'Are you in Cheshire on business, Zac?'

'No.' He hadn't taken his eyes from hers for a moment. 'I can't say I was just passing so I decided to drop in. I came especially to see you, Cindy.'

'Zac's staying to dinner,' her father put in. 'Your mother's gone to have a word with Mrs B.'

'Yes, I—I saw her just now. Well, I—I'm sorry to have kept you waiting. I've been shopping.'

'So your father told me. For a birthday present, I believe.' He was not in the least put out, not in the least uncomfortable. He leaned back and stretched his long legs before him, his arms spread across the back of the settee in an attitude which was, again, so familiar to her.

She could tell her father approved of him. Sir Robert was not easily impressed by people and he had a way of making it known when he disliked someone. 'Zac's been here a couple of hours, darling. He arrived just after lunch. We've been having an interesting conversation— shop talk.'

'Advertising?'

'Law.' Sir Robert grinned. 'Zac is very well read. Aren't you, young man?'

'A mine of information.' Zac shrugged. 'Though a lot of it's useless to me.'

Feeling obliged to say something, anything, Cindy told her father of Zac's extraordinary memory. 'He— has the ability to retain almost everything he reads.'

Cindy's mother came in then, just in time to hear what had been said. 'And we've been talking politics. We've put the world to rights.' She smiled, 'And the men have made several changes in legislation which should help matters.'

'I see.' Cindy managed to laugh, but it sounded as if it were someone else's laughter. She could hardly believe what was happening. Her parents were enchanted. Zac had obviously turned on the charm, and it had worked. She forced herself to sit back in her chair. Her limbs felt lifeless, her mouth as dry as parchment. 'Have I missed tea, Mummy?'

'No, darling. Mrs B. will be in in a minute or two. Did you have a successful shopping trip?'

Cindy nodded, her mind so blank that she'd

forgotten what she'd done with her day; all her parcels were on the back seat of her car.

'Had you planned on driving back to London tonight, Zac?' The question came from her father.

'That—depends.' Zac looked directly at Cindy and she shifted uncomfortably, hating the way he was putting some sort of onus on her. She could see what was coming next and she cursed her father for it.

'Stay the night. It'll be late by the time we've finished dinner, and fog's forecast for tonight. The motorway will be hazardous. We've got bags of room. I mean, if business permits.'

'Business,' Zac said slowly, in a voice which told Cindy he was thinking of something quite different, 'permits. That's kind of you Sir Robert. I accept.'

Her father nodded, satisfied. He'd like that, Zac's no-nonsense acceptance. Or refusal. No dithering. And she couldn't really blame him for extending the invitation. If he hadn't, her mother would have. She looked from one to the other, wondering if either of them really had any idea how difficult this was for her? Surely, surely if they had they wouldn't extend their hospitality so readily, even if it was typical of them.

Mrs B. came in with afternoon tea and during the next hour or so Zac and her parents continued to talk as if they'd known each other for years. They were still talking politics, obviously continuing the conversation which Cindy's arrival had interrupted. Both her parents were interested in politics; Cindy was not. She wasn't even up to date on current affairs—though it was not for that reason that she hardly contributed a word.

It was as if she weren't really present. She was sitting there, her *body* was sitting there, and yet she felt as if she were standing in a corner of the room, just looking on. She watched her mother watching Zac as only her mother could—shrewdly but not in the least obviously. Behind the dignified, polite composure which was the outward stamp of her mother's personality there was a sharp, intelligent woman who was an extremely good judge of character. From Cindy she had heard quite a lot about Zac Stone in the early days of his takeover of Bryant's—little of which had been complimentary—and now she was judging for herself.

Cindy looked at her watch, knowing what was about to happen. Her parents were creatures of habit, always had been as far as domestic routine was concerned. But she hoped against hope that they would make an exception today. She was dreading the moment when she would find herself alone with Zac.

They didn't make an exception today, and her mother spoke first. 'Bobby darling, it's four o'clock.'

'Just a minute, Pamela.' Sir Robert held up a hand, turning to his guest. 'There's a flaw in your thinking, young man. You don't seem to have understood my last point. If you consider——'

'Hold on.' Zac suppressed a smile, shook his head lazily. 'I've followed your argument all right. But five minutes ago you asked me to accept an assumption. What you're saying makes sense, but it's based on a premise I don't agree with.'

'Bobby , , ,' Pamela Hetherington got to her feet and put her own full stop on the argument. 'Forgive us, Zac, but we always take a rest during the afternoon. Cindy will look after you, and it'll give you a chance to talk.'

'What? Oh, yes.' His wife's last sentence prompted Sir Robert into action. He got to his feet. 'Doctor's orders. I'm supposed to rest during the afternoon.' Then, with a mixture of amusement and irritation he added, 'we'll sort this one out over dinner, Zac.'

'I'll look forward to it,' the younger man grinned.

When her parents went out the silence between Cindy and Zac swept across the room like a heavy velvet curtain might sweep across the stage in a theatre. They were like strangers; strangers who had shared so much intimacy but knew one another hardly at all. He looked different suddenly. Perhaps it was because he was no longer engrossed in conversation, perhaps it was because Cindy had hardly dared to look at him properly during the last hour, being too acutely aware that he was watching her even while he kept up the chatter with her parents. He looked a little older, strained, and the tension which might have been present earlier was stealing its way into his body. Almost imperceptibly, but it was there.

'Hello, Goldilocks.' The deep voice was quiet, neutral, the two words being used as a thermometer to measure her reaction now she was without the support, or hindrance, of her parents' presence.

She had an overwhelming desire to cry, to accuse, to tell him to leave so that she might achieve once again the inner calm she had known only that morning, the inner calm it had taken her three months to achieve. 'What—what do you want?'

'You.'

Irrationally her heartbeat accelerated. She called herself every kind of fool for momentarily misinterpreting the single word. 'You haven't found another secretary?'

'Yes.' His eyes refused her the luxury of looking away. 'And no. When I got your letter I hired someone straight away. She lasted half a day. So I got someone else.'

'And?'

'And she lasted two minutes.'

Sheila sprang to mind. At least Cindy had lasted more than two minutes. She laughed shortly, hollowly, to release the tension inside her. 'It isn't everyone who can work for you, Zac. But you know that.'

'I made two errors of judgment.'

'That doesn't sound like you.' The remark surprised her. 'Have you got someone now?'

'No. I've—managed. With Alison, with some help from Greg's secretary.'

'How are things going?' Cindy was trying hard to be casual. They had, after all, parted on good terms. They hadn't fought. And he had no idea how much the Tracy

Lynn business had hurt her—because he had no idea how much she cared. 'How ... how's the Germaine launch coming along?'

'We've finished work on that.' He said it impatiently, as if he were glad it was out of the way. 'The first ads are due to be televised this weekend.'

'Really?' Cindy couldn't help being impressed, but she shuddered to think what life had been like at Bryant's during the past three months. Maybe that was why Zac looked so strained ... 'I'm—what can I say? Congratulations.' He had wanted to launch the new range before Christmas and it had been a tall order— but he had succeeded. Of course he had succeeded. She wondered whether Tracy would appear in the ad, but it was more than she could do to ask the question. The thought of the other woman made her voice come out harshly. 'Well, if you're here to ask me back to Bryant's, forget it. I've no intention of coming back. I have little interest in the ad world at all.'

An odd expression flitted across his face. It was something she couldn't interpret, a look she had never seen before. It was almost approaching ... sadness. She reproached herself instantly. What a fanciful idea! Maybe he was disappointed, but that was all. Crisply she added, 'If you'd thought it might be necessary to try and coax me back you'd have answered my letter, I suppose.'

Zac got up, moved around restlessly before sitting in the window seat. He turned, looking out of the window so she was unable to see his face. 'I have little interest in the ad world, too.'

Cindy stared at him, wishing she could see his eyes so she might understand him better. Was this some sort of tactic, a way of persuading her back to work? But no, that wasn't his style. He didn't use those sort of tactics. As if to prove her right he said, 'I want you back, Cindy. I—didn't know how to answer your letter. It was so final. I made several attempts at a reply and I discarded them all.' He turned suddenly, making her jump inwardly as if he'd touched every inch of her. 'This morning I saw the porter letting himself into your flat. When I asked what the devil he was doing, he said you'd sent him your key—asked him to make arrangements to have all your stuff removed. I'd like to know your intentions, Cindy. Why aren't you coming back to London? Your father's long since recovered, and I know you well enough to realise you must be bored here.'

His eyes swept around the room, a rather dreary room with its heavy brown curtains, its tapestries and antiques. 'What are you doing here? I realise this place is home, but it just isn't you. This place is like a mausoleum! You must feel suffocated, in spite of its size.'

She smiled because she knew what he meant. It was a gross exaggeration, but she could see his point. 'I am. Coming back to London, I mean.'

If she'd doubted it before, she knew then she was in danger. In two strides Zac crossed the room, took hold of her by the elbows and pulled her roughly to her feet. 'Then why are you leaving the flat?' he demanded. 'What have I done that you can't bear to live next door to me when you get back?'

'Zac, don't——'

'What are you afraid of? This?'

She was lost, as she'd known she would be, immediately he touched her. But when he kissed her she fought him with everything in her, fought before she drowned in the all-consuming passion she felt for him. It served only to inflame him, with anger as well as arousal. He laughed scornfully as she pulled her head away, catching her flailing arms and holding them effortlessly behind her. The movement pulled her against the length of his body, and she knew he'd never stopped wanting her, as she'd never stopped wanting him. No matter how many women he had made love to since Paris, he still wanted her. She was still a challenge to him.

He kissed her savagely until her lips parted beneath his and she was kissing him back. She returned his kiss because she had no choice. She had never known how to resist him. And he would not allow her her freedom until he had demonstrated again that she was his for the taking.

'You see?' His lips moved over her face, down her neck, pausing in the hollow at the base of her throat.

'You see why you have to come back to me? You're mine, Cindy. We have unfinished business . . .'

She gasped as he bit softly into her shoulder, pulling aside the fine wool of her dress. 'I hate you,' she frowned. 'I hate you for coming here. I hate you for doing this to me——'

'Do you?' his eyes mocked her. 'You know what hatred's akin to, don't you?'

She should have known words were no longer a defence, should have known she had no defences left. Zac's hands moved over her hips, into the curve of her spine, bringing her body against his own with the grace and fluidity of a wave. As his hands cupped her breasts, he cursed suddenly, moving away from her abruptly and turning his back.

Stupidly, uncomprehendingly, she blinked and then spun around as she heard the sound of someone clearing their throat. Mrs B. stood in the doorway, her embarrassment equalling Cindy's.

'I'm sorry. I——'

If she'd knocked, Cindy hadn't heard it. But Zac had.

'I'm sorry, Miss Cynthia, but there was a telephone call for your mother and of course she's——'

'Yes? What is it, Mrs B.?' Cindy spoke more sharply to her than she had ever done.

'Dr Trent's wife. She has an unexpected visitor and wondered whether she should cancel the arrangements for tomorrow night or whether she might bring her visitor with her. I—I thought you might like to ring her back, only she's going out shortly.'

'Yes. Right away.'

Mrs Butterworth backtracked at once, and Zac swore again immediately the door was closed. 'I've got an overnight case in the car, Cindy. Show me my room before you make that call. I'll get my case.'

She went out with him to the cars and collected her parcels. Walking up the sweeping staircase ahead of him, she could feel his eyes on her with every step she took. 'You—you should be comfortable in here, Zac.' She opened the door to one of the guestrooms. 'I'll make that phone call and see you in the conservatory. We—we can talk in there.'

But what else was there to say? How was she going to cope with him during the remaining hours before dinner? With trembling hands she picked up the telephone in her bedroom and dialled Mrs Trent's number.

In the middle of her conversation her bedroom door opened and Zac stepped in. Cindy almost jumped off the bed, holding the receiver with both hands for fear she might drop it. 'Yes, yes I'm qu-quite sure.' Stammering, almost deafened to what she was hearing, she saw Zac turn the key in the lock and walk slowly towards her. She closed her fingers over the mouthpiece as his hands spanned her waist and he pulled her down beside him on the bed. 'Get out of here! ... Sorry? No, no trouble at all. My parents will be delighted.' She closed her eyes, swaying involuntarily against Zac as he brushed her hair aside and kissed the nape of her neck, the palms of his hands moving ever so lightly over the tips of her breasts.

With a hasty farewell she dropped the receiver into its cradle and stilled the movement of his hands. 'Zac, please——'

'That's all right,' he murmured against her ear. 'We won't have any more interruptions. The door's locked.'

'For heaven's sake, not here! Not here, in this house!' She pulled away sharply, putting distance between them.

He made no move to come after her. 'Then where? When?'

Cindy swallowed hard, looking away from him, defeated. 'I—we'll leave in the morning. We can—can book into a hotel if you like.' Though she wasn't looking at him, she was aware of his every movement. He stretched out on the bed, his broad shoulders pushing the pillows into a comfortable position, the sheer size of him making her bed, and her room, seem smaller.

'I like.' There was the sudden flash of white which was his smile. Very quietly he added, 'So I finally have your acquiescence, Cindy.'

'My—what?' She had no idea what he meant. Then she remembered their fraught conversation in Paris. 'Oh, I see.' She looked at him levelly. 'Yes, you have my acquiescence. And if you're interested, I won't hate myself in the morning.'

He was very still, watching her eyes. 'And why is that? What's changed?'

At the threat of tears, Cindy's hands curled into fists, her nails digging into her palms. If she cried, he would know. He would know how she felt. 'I've changed. I want you. It's as simple as that.'

The silence screamed at her. She was aware of her own heartbeat, aware of the soft pitter-patter of the rain on the windows, but the silence before he spoke was an agony.

'You wanted me before. You haven't answered my question. What's changed?'

'I——' She floundered before reasserting herself. 'I've had a lot of time to think—about all sorts of things. I no longer see any reason for resisting a physical attraction.' Almost defiantly, though she was unaware of it, her head came up. 'I've told you, my attitude towards that subject has changed.'

He was looking at her now with eyes which had narrowed. He was discounting every sentence she spoke. He didn't believe her. Worse than that, he knew.

He knew how she felt and he was pinning her down deliberately. It was some sort of sadistic game. She felt her stomach turn sickeningly.

'So you're willing to have an affair with me?' he raised an eyebrow. 'You're telling me this in the cold light of day, quite dispassionately?'

'Yes,' she whispered, 'I am.' As her mouth closed she bit hard into her cheeks, willing herself not to cry.

'Now ...' At his tone, she braced herself. He had caught his prey and he was playing with her mercilessly. '... Can you look me in the eyes and tell me you'll be *content* to have an affair with me?'

The first humiliating tears spilled on to her lashes. 'No.'

He went in for the kill very gently. Almost inaudibly he demanded, 'And why is that?'

'Because I love you.' She said it on a sigh, the tears spilling over on to her cheeks. Then her breath caught on a sob and she turned her back on him.

CHAPTER THIRTEEN

SHE heard no movement. But suddenly he was there, standing behind her, his arms reaching out to cradle her against him as if she were made of glass. As he turned her gently to face him, she looked into the blue, fathomless depths of his eyes. There was no laughter, no satisfaction—just a reflection of something she couldn't name because she'd never seen it before.

'Sit down, darling.' He led her to a chair, sitting facing her as she reached for a tissue and dabbed at her eyes. Unable to resist in any way she let him take it from her and wipe away her tears. 'You haven't changed, Cindy. Oh, maybe you've grown more tolerant, more understanding of other people, but you're basically the same. It's I who's changed, not you. You don't want an affair with me now any more than you ever did. And I'm glad, because I don't want an affair with you.'

Startled by his words, she looked at him in disbelief, her brown eyes dark with bewilderment.

'I love you,' he said simply. 'I don't want you to come back as my secretary, I want you to be my wife.'

'Zac——' It wasn't a game. Over and over she told herself this wasn't a game, that he meant what he'd said. But she couldn't believe what was happening, couldn't cope with the sheer joy that pervaded her being. Nor could she speak.

'Why did you leave me?' There was a note of pleading in his voice, something else which was totally alien to her—to him. 'Why did you put me through such hell for so long?'

'Tracy——' Her eyes closed against fresh tears. 'I couldn't cope with—with that.'

For a split second Zac looked blank, then confused.

He took hold of her hands. 'Tracy Lynn? But what—what's she got to do with us?'

It didn't matter to Cindy any more. She wanted Zac regardless. Regardless of what he was or was not, regardless of what he'd done. So she shrugged her slender shoulders. 'You made love to her, the weekend I left London. But it doesn't matter. Not now. I understood it even as I hated it. But I couldn't blame you. Not after . . . after Paris.'

Zac let go of her hand, got swiftly to his feet. 'Dear God, I don't believe this!'

'It doesn't matter. Zac, it——'

'It matters.' Tiredly he ran a hand through his hair. 'To think I've——'

He stopped abruptly. A cold fear crept inside Cindy as she wished fervently that she'd never mentioned Tracy Lynn.

'You saw her?' he asked wearily. 'On the Monday morning, when you were leaving to go to the hospital?'

'Yes.'

'And you thought I'd spent the night making love to her? With you lying in your own bed on the other side of the wall?'

'Yes.'

'Dear God! No wonder you didn't come back! I didn't make love to her, Cindy. I never even thought about it!' He turned to face her, his eyes locking on to hers. 'You don't believe me.'

'It doesn't matter——'

'Have I ever lied to you? Forget everything else I've done to you and answer me that.'

'No. But she said—she said you and she had overslept that morning. What—what was I supposed to think?' Incredibly he was making her feel guilty. 'Zac, I'm sorry, but I thought you'd turned to Tracy . . . I mean, after Paris you never tried . . . After Paris——'

He nodded, a wry smile pulling at his lips as though he understood, now, everything. 'Paris . . .' He sat, laughing shortly, humourlessly. 'I'd better explain what happened to me in Paris. Darling Cindy, discovering your virginity wasn't the only shock I had in Paris. I discovered that I loved you—that for the first time in my life, I was in love. And I discovered that my days at Bryant's would be numbered, that the challenge I'd come out of retirement to find was an empty one—too easy, unreal. When I got the phone call from Alain, telling me we had the Germaine business, I realised in that moment that it wasn't work which was making me happy. It was you. I'd landed the Germaine account against all the odds; it was possibly the biggest coup of my career . . . and a hollow victory.'

Cindy closed her eyes, recalling the scene, the way he had responded so strangely to the news. She nodded slowly. 'Your reputation goes before you, as I once told you. And it works for you so much that——'

'That nothing is impossibly difficult now. I don't give a hoot. I want you, Cindy. I want children. I want time to spend with my wife and my family. I'm extricating myself from Bryant's. The Germaine launch is done, and I've been scouting round for someone who'll buy into the agency. Greg Halliday would like to hold the reins, and the way I'm feeling right now, I'd make him a gift of my shares.'

She laughed at him. 'But you won't—I mean, make him a gift.'

'Of course not,' he grinned. 'I haven't changed that much. Not quite.' The laughter faded from his eyes. 'but I've changed a great deal since I met you, Cindy. You know, in the past I've never hesitated to take what I want. With you, I couldn't. I couldn't take what you were unprepared to give, to give willingly, with your heart, your mind, as well as your body. After Paris I waited for you to come to me. Two weeks, Cindy. Two weeks passed and you avoided even coming for a drink with me. I thought it was hopeless. You'd denied it, but I was convinced you'd been saving yourself for someone very special, and I knew it wasn't me. You were mine for the taking . . . but I couldn't take that from you.

'After you left—when I got your letter—I fought with myself daily not to ring you, to come after you. I had no idea that you cared. Do you see that? I only discovered what you felt for me when you walked into the drawing room this afternoon.' Smiling, he reached for her hands. 'My cool, level-headed darling! Your composure had slipped. I knew what you were feeling, because I recognised the symptoms. I felt it, too. I've been unbearable to work with these past weeks. I've even bawled at Greg. I—when I saw them taking your furniture away, I—I can't tell you how I felt. I'd been waiting for you to come home—not to Bryant's, but home. When I learnt that you weren't coming back I got straight into the car and drove up here. The realisation that you were disappearing completely brought me to my senses. I came to ask you to marry me. Cindy, you're all that matters in the world to me.'

He broke off, turning the palms of her hands upwards and kissing them tenderly. 'I've found a house in the country. You'll love it, darling, I'm sure. It's perfect for us. It has a rose garden and an orchard, extensive grounds. I left a deposit on it some time ago, but I—I've done nothing about it since. If you like it, it's yours. Will you marry me, darling?'

Cindy reached for him, locking her arms around his neck as he pulled her on to his lap. 'Yes, I'll marry you, my love. Just as you are! Changed, unchanged——' She lifted her face for his kiss, a kiss which spoke of tenderness, caring . . .

'Cindy, how many men have you made love to since you left London?'

She didn't even bother to answer that one!

Zac's eyes danced with amusement. 'Precisely. And that's why I didn't make love to Tracy. She was quite willing to be . . . persuaded . . . into doing the Germaine job. But her price was too high—far too high. She's got herself a boy-friend. He's married, wealthy, and possessive enough for him not to want her to model any more.'

The broad shoulders lifted in a shrug. 'When I took her to dinner on the Friday, she said maybe. But I didn't know why she was hesitating. She'd have made a lot of money from doing the ad. We made a date for the Sunday evening and when I took her home for a nightcap, she asked me if she were staying the night. I said no.'

'I don't quite follow, Zac. I take it her boy-friend keeps her. Did she think you might be a replacement for him?'

'Something like that. And I've no doubt I would have picked up where our relationship left off . . . if I hadn't met you. We talked, she and I. You must remember we were friends in the past, as well as lovers. We talked well into the night, catching up on the past two years—though she did most of the talking. She told me what she'd been doing, about her boy-friend and how they met. . . .'

'And then?'

'And then I kissed her goodnight—and all the time I was thinking about you. You can believe it or not, Cindy; I put her in the spare room. She looked at me as if she'd never seen me before. "Who is it, Zac?" she said. She teased me mercilessly. "I've told you everything and you've told me nothing! Who is it that's wheedled her way into that ruthless heart of yours?" I went into my own room in a kind of . . . shock. Kissing Tracy was absolutely meaningless.'

He let out a long, slow breath, shaking his head as if he still couldn't believe what had happened to him. 'I don't have your morals, Cindy. And I'm far less scrupulous than you—but if that night with Tracy Lynn is anything to go by I can safely say I'm yours . . . faithfully.'

'Oh, Zac, Zac! All I ask is that you love me.' She nuzzled against his neck, feeling their hearts beating in unison as he held her tightly against him. 'Just make me feel secure in your love.'

'That's easy enough,' he murmured, as he kissed her tear-filled eyes.

Harlequin® |Plus|

THE FINE WHISKY OF SCOTLAND

More than five hundred years ago, Scotch whisky was the he-man's drink of Scotland's common folk. The companion to hard toil and exercise in the clear Highland air, *uisgebeatha* — Gaelic for "water of life" — was also the only drink served at weddings and wakes, and the *deoch an dorius*—"final door drink"—at parties.

In the Highlands of Scotland, among the misty mountains, the dark still lakes and the untamed rivers, the unique ingredients that go into the manufacture of Scotch whisky are found. Here the barley for the malt is grown, then sprouted for several days in water that has acquired a brownish color from flowing through the rich dark peat moss on the moors. The sprouted barley is then dried in a peat fire, and it is the acrid and oily smoke that gives the whisky its characteristic aroma. The dried sprouts are mashed into a grist and soaked in hot water, producing a malt. When the water, or *wort*, has absorbed all the goodness of the malt, it is drained and fermented into beer. The beer is fermented three more times—during which process it is changed to a wine, then distilled to a liquor — before being drawn into casks and aged for anywhere from three to ten years.

When Welshman Zac, the hero of Claudia Jameson's novel, sits down to enjoy a glass of his favorite drink he perhaps heeds the advice of this Scottish saying: "There are two things a Scotsman likes naked, and one of them is Scotch." It is only by sipping Scotch whisky straight that one can fully enjoy the light smoky malt flavor that makes this liquor world renowned.

Experience the warmth of…

Harlequin Romance

**The original romance novels.
Best-sellers for more than 30 years.**

Delightful and intriguing love stories
by the world's foremost writers
of romance fiction.

Be whisked away to dazzling
international capitals…
or quaint European villages.
Experience the joys of falling in love…
for the first time, the best time!

Harlequin Romance

**A uniquely absorbing journey
into a world of superb romance reading.**

**No one touches the heart of a woman
quite like Harlequin!**

4 FREE

Harlequin Romances

Get all the latest books before they're sold out!

As a Harlequin subscriber you actually receive your personal copies of the latest Romances immediately after they come off the press, so you're sure of getting all 6 each month.

Cancel your subscription whenever you wish!

You don't have to buy any minimum number of books. Whenever you decide to stop your subscription just let us know and we'll cancel all further shipments.

Your FREE gift includes

- MAN OF POWER by **Mary Wibberley**
- THE WINDS OF WINTER by **Sandra Field**
- THE LEO MAN by **Rebecca Stratton**
- LOVE BEYOND REASON by **Karen van der Zee**

FREE GIFT CERTIFICATE

and Subscription Reservation
Mail this coupon today!

Harlequin Reader Service

In the U.S.A.	In Canada
1440 South Priest Drive	649 Ontario Street
Tempe, AZ 85281	Stratford, Ontario N5A 6W2

Please send me my 4 Harlequin Romance novels FREE.
Also, reserve a subscription to the 6 NEW Harlequin
Romance novels published each month. Each month I will
receive 6 NEW Romance novels at the low price of $1.50
each (*Total–$9.00 a month*). There are no shipping and
handling or any other hidden charges. I may cancel this
arrangement at any time, but even if I do, these first 4 books
are still mine to keep.

_____

NAME   (PLEASE PRINT)

_____

ADDRESS   APT. NO.

_____

CITY

_____

STATE/PROV.   ZIP/POSTAL CODE
Offer not valid to present subscribers
Offer expires July 31, 1984   116 BPR EAN3

If price changes are necessary you will be notified.